She'd been shot at twice in one day.

This time, she heard the pop of gunfire right before the window shattered. She fell to the floor.

"Adriana!" Levi called out, and she felt his weight pressing on her, sheltering her.

More bullets flew. She didn't know how many. The shots were loud, echoing. She huddled closer to the couch, desperate for some kind of cover.

"We've got to crawl to the other room." Levi's voice was breathless. "Ready? Go." He lifted himself up and they crawled together. Even as they stopped in the kitchen, she felt as if her heart was running away from her chest at a dead sprint toward somewhere far from bullets and bodies in lakes.

"Who is doing this?" she cried.

"The serial killer. Or someone doing his dirty work."

Whoever was after Levi was monstrous, Adriana realized. Completely monstrous.

And by offering to help track down the killer, she'd put herself right in his path.

Sarah Varland lives in Alaska with her husband, John, their two boys and their dogs. Her passion for books comes from her mom; her love for suspense comes from her dad, who has spent a career in law enforcement. When she's not writing, she's often found dog mushing, hiking, reading, kayaking, drinking coffee or enjoying other Alaskan adventures with her family.

Books by Sarah Varland

Love Inspired Suspense

Treasure Point Secrets
Tundra Threat
Cold Case Witness
Silent Night Shadows
Perilous Homecoming
Mountain Refuge
Alaskan Hideout
Alaskan Ambush
Alaskan Christmas Cold Case
Alaskan Showdown

Visit the Author Profile page at Harlequin.com.

ALASKAN SHOWDOWN

SARAH VARLAND

LOVE INSPIRED SUSPENSE

INSPIRATIONAL ROMANCE

LOVE INSPIRED® SUSPENSE
INSPIRATIONAL ROMANCE

ISBN-13: 978-1-335-57460-2

Alaskan Showdown

Copyright © 2020 by Sarah Varland

Love Inspired
22 Adelaide St. West, 40th Floor
Toronto, Ontario M5H 4E3, Canada
www.Harlequin.com

Printed in U.S.A.

Trust in the Lord with all thine heart;
and lean not unto thine own understanding. In all
thy ways acknowledge him, and he shall direct thy paths.
–Proverbs 3:5-6

To wilderness search-and-rescue workers,
unsung backcountry heroes. Thank you for all you do.

ONE

They'd been searching for the missing twenty-something hiker for days and Adriana Steele had thought this time all was going to turn out well, that maybe they'd have that happy ending that search-and-rescue teams dreamed of.

Then she had climbed into the boat with her dog, Blue, and Blue had come to alert in the middle of Haven Lake.

Not the alert she used for people who were still alive. Blue did search and rescue—that was why she'd brought her along—but she was also the best cadaver dog she'd had the privilege of working with. One of the only ones she knew of who was able to sniff out the decay of a body, even when it was underwater. She'd done it before.

And that was her signal. Someone was dead.

Adriana had radioed the discovery in to the dive team, who had been waiting, and navigated her search boat back to the lakeshore.

She had done her best to push past the clench of pain in her chest. She knew what the family was going to go through now from personal experience. Saving people made facing her own personal demons worth it, but she paid a heavy price every time there was someone she couldn't rescue.

Blue whined. Adriana reached down and petted her behind the ears. Finding people took a toll on the dog, too.

She waited with her at their truck, sat right there on the tailgate and watched the activity. The team had recovered the body from the lake, and law enforcement was over there with the search-and-rescue team members who had stayed in the immediate vicinity. The last thing Adriana had heard before she walked away, far enough away to give her some emotional distance, was that the body matched the description of Lara Jones, a hiker who had disappeared from nearby earlier in the week. A roommate had reported her missing, no foul play had been suspected before now and her car was parked at a trailhead not far from the lake.

It was tragic, but familiar. These cases happened too often, where hikers went missing and ended up dead, from some accident or another, enough times that Adriana knew how this worked. Someone was going to have to give a statement and since Adriana had found the body— well, her dog had—they'd want to talk to her specifically.

As long as it was a reasonable individual, she'd be fine. As long as it wasn't... No, she pushed aside the thought.

It's just there was one officer she'd rather not work with.

At this point, though, she'd talk to anyone if she could just get out of here. She could only hold it together for so many more minutes. She and Blue both needed to decompress. Maybe go for a run.

Adriana looked toward the group that had gathered around the body covered with a sheet.

She swallowed hard.

The landscape morphed. She no longer saw the fall leaves, changing on the trees from dull green to browns, golds and reds. Instead she saw winter in her mind. A lake like this, but frozen over. A recovered snow machine.

We're sorry, but he went through the ice and didn't make it...

Adriana stood so fast her head spun, dizziness making her weak.

She sat back down, reaching her hand out to steady herself.

"Whoa, are you okay?"

Levi Wicks grabbed her arm. He was the last person she wanted to see here. Well, maybe second to last. At least Levi gave some kind of credence to the idea of using dogs in search-and-rescue teams, even to assist law enforcement, whereas his brother thought they did no good at all. No, it wasn't that part of Levi that bothered her. He was a laid-back "good old boy," as they'd have called him where she was from, easygoing and unconcerned. Nothing flustered him. Nothing made him upset.

Adriana didn't understand him. Being easily invested emotionally—wasn't that part of what made her such a good search-and-rescue team member?

At the moment, though, he was all that was between her and passing out, maybe hitting her head on a rock on her way to the ground, so she should probably be a little more forgiving of his personality flaws.

"Adriana? Can you hear me?"

Yes, she could hear him. She was having a panic attack; she wasn't deaf. But when she opened her mouth to answer, nothing came out. Anxiety choked her, cut off her airway, and she started to see spots again.

Not now.

But panic and the past never listened to her, never stayed where they belonged stuffed deep down inside, behind all the other thoughts and feelings she had. No, they had to intrude, unannounced and very much uninvited on days like today.

We can recover his body, but he's gone, Adriana.

Her first love. Only love. Taken by a lake like this.

Adriana felt her eyes fill and for a horrible minute thought she might cry in front of this man. He was certainly the *last* person she'd want to cry in front of, not even second to last. How could someone like him possibly understand her feelings?

Besides, she'd never cried about Robert's death. Not in the entire five years since it had happened.

She certainly wasn't going to start now.

"Adriana." She felt his weight settle beside her on the tailgate and blinked several times to clear her vision, to banish memories of the past and remind herself that she wasn't back there, that today wasn't *that* day. She needed to remind herself *these* feelings needed to stay buried at the bottom of her heart, where they belonged.

Her head spun and she squeezed her eyes shut, feeling herself start to give up on talking herself down from this attack. Maybe it was better to just let the emotions come, awful as it would be. She couldn't fix it, couldn't change the past.

She felt Levi's arm brush against her back, then her shoulder, and come to rest on her upper arm.

"Hey." He pulled her close to him. "You did your best. It's an awful way to die and I'm sorry you had to see it."

He was talking about today, and the body. Adriana knew that. But he didn't know about Robert. Couldn't know…

"It's not that." She heard her voice, watery though it was.

"Other…?" He trailed off. "Bad memories?"

Was that his voice breaking? Almost like he was fighting emotions of his own?

Adriana took a breath, steadied somehow by his unsteadiness.

"My fiancé drowned. Five years ago."

No. No. No. She heard her voice. Yes, that was *her* that had said that. She'd carried the secret with her from Wasilla, where she'd lived before "the accident," as all their friends called it in hushed tones. Then she'd moved to Anchorage, taken some search-and-rescue classes, given up her work as a dog trainer and moved to Raven Pass to work with the team.

And she'd not told a soul why until now.

"You are the strongest woman I know." His voice was still rough around the edges, heavy with something that made Adriana realize she wasn't the only one with old hurts.

He might have only just found out. They might not be close at all.

But he understood. And somehow, right now, it felt like enough.

For the first time in five years, Adriana started to sob.

"I couldn't save him."

He pulled her closer.

"You can't save them all."

Officer Levi Wicks hated failure with every fiber of his being. Especially when he wasn't ready to quit on something and giving up was forced on him, the decision taken out of his hands.

Sorry, Officer Wicks. There's just not enough to keep the case open.

His chief's words from the night before played again in his mind as he held Adriana while she cried. He'd finished his shift and kept his mind on patrol—the people of Raven Pass didn't deserve a distracted law enforcement officer—but once his shift had ended he hadn't been able to stop thinking about the serial-killer case that had occupied all his spare moments for the last few years.

Probably it would have helped if he'd left the police department and gone home, but to do that would be to admit that the last few years of work were really over and had come to nothing.

Levi hadn't worked exclusively on a single case for the last several years. It was a small department, so there was a lot of multitasking, but when he could he'd been looking into the most recent string of unexplained murders in the area. Two deaths had taken place in Raven Pass, with a third in nearby Girdwood. There'd been a fourth farther down on the Kenai Peninsula in the town of Hope, ironically enough.

This case hadn't been his only. But it had occupied enough space in his mind over the last few years that it felt fully like *his* case.

Levi had been on this assignment since his second year in the department. He'd worked it with his partner, Jim Johnson, straight through until Jim's retirement last spring.

He was letting Jim down. Letting the victims' families down. They deserved closure.

The night before, he'd been heading for his truck, ready to head home, but turned around and walked instead to the cold-case room.

The door was cold and the handle opened easily after Levi had unlocked it. He'd signed in on the clipboard that hung by the door and stepped into the room, which felt cooler than the hallway had been. That made sense. The evidence related to these cases was stored here to avoid decomposition.

Pieces of peoples' lives, those odd discordant details that reminded him that nothing about his job was natural. Levi and his brother Judah had both become police officers to deal with the darkness in the world. Their eldest brother, Ryan, had become a pastor.

He supposed everyone had their ways of coping with the broken world they lived in.

Every box in the room represented a cop who hadn't been able to do his job, who'd walked away feeling like Levi was.

He hadn't known why he was there exactly, but still he'd walked around the room, removing a box here and there, looking through the case files, setting them back down.

It was all he'd been able to think to do at the time.

The next box had been a missing-persons case. It had gone cold in 1977, not long after the Raven Pass PD had been established. A man, midthirties at the time, had gone hiking and never been seen again.

Heaviness had settled on him again, so he'd set the lid on top of that box and slid it back onto the shelf.

He'd needed to leave and do something to get his mind off his work. It wasn't like him to wallow in a sense of melancholy.

As he had walked toward the door, Levi took one last look behind him, imagining his case on these shelves.

Then one more box had caught his eye. The label was faded, the edges peeling slightly.

Women in Their Twenties. Twenty Years Ago.
Serial Killer.

He'd slid the box off the shelf.

It stung, how many criminals were never found and brought to justice.

Levi had settled the box on the table. Opened it.

The first folder was about a girl named Jessica. Average height, he had noted, taking in the features on the photograph of her like this case wasn't colder than ice itself. Blond hair, past her shoulders. She looked friendly. Pretty.

She'd been killed at twenty-two and found on a popular hiking trail near Anchorage. Investigation had revealed that she'd been killed near Raven Pass.

The folder had slid back into the box easily and Levi had grabbed the next one. Its details were similar to the first, except this one specifically mentioned that the victim had been abducted from a coffee shop. Just like the victims in his case over the past three years. All women in their twenties. Usually early twenties. Bodies found buried.

He'd swallowed hard. There were a lot of coffee shops in Alaska. Had anyone at the department worked there for more than two decades? Levi hadn't thought so.

Still, he wouldn't know if there was significance to what he'd found until he looked at the next folder.

Another woman. Annie. Disappeared from a coffee shop. Presumed dead.

Chills had run down his arms, down his spine.

And last night's realizations hit him all over again.

The women in the case he'd been working had all disappeared from coffee shops…

Either someone knew of this case and was copycatting…

Or the killer had stopped for more than a decade and then started again.

And Levi thought this body might be another one of his victims.

* * *

Levi shook himself from his memories to the crying woman he still held in his arms. He was in way deeper here than he'd meant to be. He'd only meant to check in at the scene that had been causing chatter on the police scanners to go crazy. When a body was discovered, it wasn't something that required multiple police officers. Levi could have let someone else handle it, but something had told him to go down there.

But when he'd gotten there and seen the state of the body, he'd known.

It was another death related to the serial killer.

The zip ties around the hands were the same. Levi was willing to bet the victim hadn't died from drowning at all, but rather had been suffocated somewhere else, like the others, and then moved.

But if she'd been a missing hiker, then she didn't fit the profile of his victims, since she hadn't been taken from a coffee shop. Her age was right. Her general build was right—most of the women killed had been medium height and weight. Could a serial killer deviate that much from his preferred MO?

And if so, why?

More than anyone else on the team, aside from his buddy Jake—who was out of town on his honeymoon—Levi trusted Adriana Steele to shoot straight with him. The woman didn't know what it was to step lightly around a subject. When you went to her, you got the truth. So he'd left the busy scene at the water's edge, where other law enforcement agents had gathered, and trekked around the lake a bit to where he saw Adriana sitting by her truck with her dog.

Alone. With a look on her face that almost made her seem…

Human. Breakable.

Even so, he hadn't expected to find her on the edge of falling apart, so needing her information for his case had taken a back seat.

Levi had never seen her like this and if

someone had asked him if he could picture her anything other than in control and too bossy for her own good, he'd have said no.

But here they were.

Adriana let out one more shuddering cry and then took a deep breath.

"I didn't want to save them all, I only want to be able to go back and save him."

Her voice came out in sobs, but Levi knew better than to believe the words. She was more like him than he'd realized. It hurt—every person he couldn't find justice for, every person he couldn't save by preventing their death. Sometimes he wondered why he'd chosen this job, what made him face that kind of defeat over and over.

He didn't always have answers for himself.

"You can't." Levi didn't try to soften the words—she wasn't the type who would appreciate that. Instead he held her higher, close enough that he could smell the berry-scented shampoo she used. Close enough to almost be able to feel her heart beating against his chest.

Levi swallowed hard. He hadn't held anyone like this in years. Hadn't wanted to.

Now...

He wished Adriana wasn't upset and would give anything to fix her pain, but the idea of her in his arms... He didn't hate it.

He should hate it. They were nothing alike.

Everything had been normal and now something in his mind, his heart, had shifted.

Please don't let me mess up everything between us for work's sake, God. Levi breathed out the prayer and inhaled again, begging for strength he wasn't sure he had to act completely normal. The words felt funny, like rusted metal trying to work again. His relationship with God was...

Well, he had one. Some days that was all he could say about it.

Long minutes passed. She kept crying.

And then she finally stopped and looked up at him with her brown eyes wide.

"I'm sorry. I've never... I don't usually..." She cleared her throat, brushed at her tears, looked away. "I'm sorry."

"You don't have to apologize. Tears aren't a crime, Adriana."

She looked up at him and there he was, staring into those eyes again, uncomfortable awareness coursing through him.

Movement to the left caught his attention. He broke eye contact and looked that way.

Just as a bullet whizzed into the ground, a foot or two from their feet. Closer to Levi's.

"Behind the truck!" he yelled at her, pulling her with him as he ran for cover. She pushed away.

"Blue!" she shouted. The dog followed and she sped up again, her speed matching Levi's. They dove behind the truck and Levi pulled her and the dog close.

"You okay, buddy? It's okay. Such a rough day, sweetheart."

Her voice was thick and sweet, like fresh honey. Of course, she would talk to her dog that way, even after someone had shot at them.

Though he'd never heard her talk to people without a little more spice in her tone.

Another shot. Across the lake, he could see the incident team taking cover also, even though the shots weren't near them. Good. They were following protocol.

Though if Levi had to guess based on the proximity to his shoes...

They were aimed at him.

"Why is someone shooting at you?"

Apparently it hadn't escaped Adriana's notice, either.

"I don't know."

But didn't he?

Had the killer been watching the site where he'd dropped his latest victim? Or had Levi been followed from the police department?

Neither option was good.

Another shot. This one hit the ground, too, kicking up rocks and dust.

Levi's radio crackled. "Unit thirty-four. I've found where the shooter is and I'm approaching."

Unit thirty-four was his brother.

He pulled the radio from his waist. "Unit thirty-four, this is unit thirty-seven. Approach with caution. The suspect may be our serial killer."

Radio silence for a solid ten seconds. Then a crackle. "Ten-four."

The shots stopped. Coincidence? Or was the killer on their radio frequency?

Levi slowed his breathing, started taking deeper breaths in and out and waited.

"Is it safe to move?" Adriana's voice was breathless, too.

"I wouldn't yet."

"I couldn't if I wanted to, anyway," she pointed out, some of the sassiness that had been missing earlier returning to her voice. "I can't move with your arms around me, holding me like this."

She had a point. He suddenly let her go like he'd been burned, and maybe he had been. Or could feel that he was about to be. Surely she hadn't thought his proximity was about anything more than keeping her safe. It hadn't been. He was just bothered by the fact that he felt more aware of her, was conscious of her presence, that she was an attractive, intriguing woman close to his age.

He watched her as he waited to be convinced everything was all right. She was collected now, the only traces of her earlier episode being some shadows of eye makeup around her eyes. It was faint, not too obvious, but it gave her a worn appearance.

How had she managed to be part of that recovery when she had something in her past similar enough that the memories gave her a panic attack? He hadn't been exaggerating when he'd told her she was the strongest woman he knew. He'd meant all of it.

Sometime he was going to tell her again, when he was sure she would believe him. Because it was true.

"So what now?" she asked after a minute.

"Well—" Levi began. Just then, the all clear came over the radio. "It's probably safe to leave our cover. You don't need to give any kind of statement about the shooting. I was here." He smiled wryly. "I do need a statement from you about... today."

"I'm assuming you don't mean my hysterical crying."

"The part right before that, I believe."

Adriana nodded. "Okay. That's fine. But actually I meant 'what now,' like what are you going to do about this? Someone is trying to kill you? Surely you're not going to just ignore that."

Well, when she put it that way.

"No. I'm not going to ignore it."

"So who is it?"

"I don't know."

She stared at him.

He stared back. Then looked away. Sighed.

"It's a case I'm on." That was all he could say. While he still needed to talk to the chief, a new discovery of a body connected to that case surely warranted keeping it open.

Adriana nodded. "The serial-killer case."

She shouldn't know about that. He hadn't been publicly mentioned in connection with the case in over a year, since the chief had fired the department's press secretary for giving out his and Jim's names. They'd done a good job since then in keeping coverage of the investigation from any of the press.

"I remember the article." She shrugged. "I rarely forget anything. It's a blessing." She looked away. "Sometimes."

"Yes, it's that case." Levi trusted her. Telling her wasn't against any kind of department policy—it was just smart to be wise with who knew the information. His safety depended on it.

Although apparently it was a little late for that.

She nodded. "I thought so. If I remember, not all the bodies have been recovered, isn't that correct? Like, weren't there some women who were assumed to be victims but their bodies were never recovered?" Her mind was spinning. This might be a way to help Levi out, regain some of her dignity, help families get closure in another way.

"Also correct, yes." Levi stood. "Okay, so I'll get back in touch with you about a statement for today, but I think for now—"

"I want to help you." Adriana blurted the words as they both stood, facing him straight on. "I want to help you find the bodies of those missing women in case it helps you solve the case."

Levi blinked. "I can't... The department isn't doing well financially and I can't afford to hire a consultant. I appreciate the thought, but—"

"I don't need to be paid. I'll work around my search-and-rescue schedule. I want to do this, Officer Wicks."

Come to think of it, she'd never called him Levi. He thought of her by her first name because everyone called her that, but she called him by a title. It was a good reminder that any relationship they had was strictly professional, and any further thoughts of her berry-scented hair, shiny in the sunshine, were fully and completely inappropriate.

"It's Levi," he said, which made no sense when he considered all the thoughts he'd just had about keeping professional boundaries.

But she nodded, still looking up at him. How could someone have such big innocent eyes and be knowledgeable about the ways the world could break a heart all at once? Looking at her eyes was like looking at her heart. Levi didn't want to look away. Didn't know if he should keep looking.

He felt like he knew her better from five minutes of face-to-face conversation than he'd known Melissa in all the months they'd been married.

So strange.

But with Melissa, what went wrong there had been his fault. He needed to remember that and not rush into a similar situation.

"Okay," Adriana said. "Levi. Please, let me help you."

He considered her again, thought about his brother out there in the woods risking his life. Looked down at the dog that he knew would do anything to keep Adriana safe.

Then he nodded his head down, just slightly. "Okay, I'll promise to think about it."

Her eyes narrowed like she was ready for a fight.

He tried not to smile. "Thinking about it is the best I can do."

That seemed to be enough. She nodded once. "Okay."

Then she walked to the front of the truck, opened the door for her dog and climbed in. "I'll be at my house when you're ready to talk. It doesn't matter how late—come by, okay?"

Levi nodded and then watched her drive away. When she was safely out of sight, he walked toward the other officers.

Could he do it, let her help him?

If he did, then he might be risking her safety, too.

But if he didn't he was risking the lives of countless other people who might be the serial killer's next targets.

Some days the weight of the job felt too heavy to carry. So for now, as he walked he worked on passing some of the weight back to Jesus, who'd promised to carry his burdens, and did his best to put Adriana Steele out of his mind.

Even while he wondered whether she'd somehow snuck past just his mind straight to his heart.

And whether or not she'd put herself in danger by doing so.

TWO

Even though she was fairly certain the shots had been directed at Levi, Adriana checked her rearview mirror almost as much as she paid attention to the road in front of her all the way home.

When she finally got to her little town house, she pulled her truck into the garage, then she and Blue walked into the house.

Babe, her other dog, met them at the door.

"Baby, did you have a good day?" She bent down to ruffle the animal's ears. She'd used Babe as her main dog even into this summer, when she and the Raven Pass search-and-rescue team were searching for Cassie Hawkins's missing aunt, but it had become apparent over the last couple of weeks that it was time to let Blue do more of the work and let Babe rest.

Blue and Babe sniffed at each other, what Adriana always pictured as one dog asking the other about his day. Some people would probably say she spent too much time with animals, but could she help it that animals made more sense than people?

Leaving the dogs to their greetings, she walked to the kitchen. Her stomach had started growling halfway home and she'd realized then that in the midst of the search she hadn't had much to eat today. All she could remember having was a granola bar for breakfast and a can of LaCroix sparkling water around mid-morning.

Probably not enough food to actually count as sustenance.

As she reached for the fridge handle, though, she caught a glimpse of her hand. Her skin was filthy—whether from the search itself or from being pushed to the ground by Levi, she wasn't sure, but it didn't matter.

Shower first, then food. And maybe the shower would help erase some of the embarrassment that flooded her again when she thought about Levi.

Adriana hurried up the stairs, feeling her cheeks heat up. Had she really broken down in front of him so completely? She wanted it not to be true, but it was, so she had to find a way to move on. Whatever else could be said about her, Adriana tried not to be the kind of girl who got bogged down in the past.

She frowned as she turned on the shower. Was she? She didn't think of herself that way, but was she wrong? She'd just spent the last hour or so trapped in the past in a way that she hadn't been able to overcome. Shame burned her cheeks again and she climbed into the hot shower, letting the water wash over her. She'd had panic attacks before, it wasn't like she hadn't known the whole…situation had a hold on her.

But it was controlled, right?

Suddenly Adriana wasn't sure.

She finished her shower, though she didn't know how she managed to focus when her mind kept going back to the comfort it had been to have someone to listen to her tears.

It was strange that it had been Levi. Of all the people it could have been, he was the one around whom she'd have chosen not to show any weakness.

Maybe that was why she'd been so insistent on helping him with the case he was working on. She had the skills and, as far as she was concerned, she owed him. Helping him find some of the victims he hadn't been able to include in his investigation, those women who were missing and fit the profile of the victims but whose bodies hadn't been found, would get him closer to identifying the suspect in the serial-killer case, and then maybe Adriana would feel like the field was level again.

She toweled off and got dressed, this time in yoga pants and a fleece pullover.

She didn't have any intention of leaving the house again today, and if she changed her mind she was going to pull on some tennis shoes and let people assume she'd been exercising. Or doing more SAR training. The Raven Pass Search and Rescue team had a core of full-time members, including her, but they spent part of their working hours training volunteers to make sure there were always enough people in a crisis.

Her cell phone rang just as she'd finished dressing.

Not a number she knew.

"Hello?" She felt her shoulders tense. It wasn't every day someone shot at her, or more accurately, at someone next to her. Maybe that was what was getting to her now, but seeing an unknown number made her uncomfortable.

"Adriana, it's Levi."

Oh. That would explain why she didn't have the number in her phone. She made a mental note to save it after the call. "Levi." It was the second time she'd called him by his first name. It was hard to be too formal with him after what had happened today.

"Are you doing okay?" she asked and then almost smacked herself in the face. He'd been shot at. How good a day could he really be having? Her question had been unnecessary.

"All things considered." His voice was even, no hint of mocking her somewhat ridiculous question. She felt her shoulders relax. How did he do this? She'd never had someone in her life who could talk her down from her ledges of drama...

Well, she had. And then he'd died.

She swallowed hard, tried to ignore the tightening in her throat.

"Did you need something?" she asked, trying to make sure her voice sounded casual.

"I still need to talk to you about the search today and its result." Levi almost sounded apologetic. The last thing Adriana wanted to do was make him feel bad. She sat up straighter, took a deep breath.

"I can talk whenever." She only hoped

that was true, and that she could do it without falling apart.

"Great." He paused, but something gave her the sense he wasn't quite finished. "Can I swing by your place now? I'd like to talk to you about it as soon as possible."

"There was something wrong, wasn't there?"

"I'll be at your home in ten minutes, if that works for you."

She nodded, though he couldn't see her. "Okay, ten minutes."

She ended the call after giving him her address, the churning in her stomach telling her that in ten minutes, whatever he was going to say could turn her life upside down. Maybe even more than her earlier offer to help him with his serial-killer case.

Because if he was this interested, the case of the missing—now deceased—hiker, Lara Jones, might be connected…

And if it was, she was already involved without her permission. And, somehow, for Adriana, that was harder to wrestle with. Having her life be in danger because she'd offered to help was one thing.

Knowing she might truly have been watched yesterday because she'd walked unaware into a case connected to a serial killer?

She shivered. That was terrifying.

THREE

As Levi drove down Adriana's street, he tried to figure out how to frame his questions. He'd talked to several other searchers after she'd left the scene earlier, but since she'd been the one to find the body—well, her dog had, since she'd probably correct him if he tried to give her the credit—he really wanted her perspective on Lara's death.

And there was more than that, if he was honest, he admitted as he pulled into her driveway. He was scared for her personally. Everyone involved in the search for the killer was in more danger than they'd been when they woke up this morning. With every detail he gathered, the more certain Levi was that the hiker was the latest victim of the serial killer he'd been tracking.

Even his boss had agreed. He'd called the chief after arriving at the scene, and seeing the body and the zip ties, the chief had agreed that he could have more time for this case.

But not a lot. He'd been clear that this was the last try. Levi had to make the most of it.

All of that was making him consider Adriana's offer. Another reason he'd wanted to talk to her in person. He couldn't gauge her facial expressions over the phone, or read her body language.

He suspected several other undiscovered bodies were still out there, and Adriana could help him find them. Not everyone missing had a point last seen in their case file, so there might be more women who could have gone missing from coffee shops but not been added to his list to investigate. Even though Lara hadn't disappeared from a coffee shop, Levi didn't think one deviation was enough to say that the killer had deviated from his or her MO. Rather, it suggested that killing Lara Jones might not have been preplanned. He wouldn't know till he investigated more. There were still a lot of variables. But if accepting Adriana's offer of help meant he found more of the bodies he suspected were out there, then he'd have several potential chances to catch the killer in a mistake, forensically speaking, or in relation to DNA. One mistake. That was all it would take to find the kind of evidence that could be invaluable.

Levi couldn't give up. Not yet.

He parked his squad car, climbed out and locked the doors, then walked toward Adriana's front door.

She opened it before he could knock. "Come in."

Her hair was wet—she must have showered right when she got home and he couldn't blame her for it. When he had days like this a shower was the second thing he did, the first being a really long run while he prayed and asked God why He let bad things happen to good people.

"Thanks." He stepped in and reached down to take his shoes off.

"I'm not from here. It makes sense to me in the winter when our boots are covered in snow, or mud, but during the rest of the year I figure that's what the vacuum is for." She gestured to a nice model vacuum that sat behind the front door.

Levi had grown up in Anchorage, so he understood Alaskan culture well and the way it dictated taking off shoes when entering a house.

"Thanks for letting me come over," he said, not sure how to fill the awkward silence. His mind was tangled already because she was even prettier than she'd been earlier and he'd never noticed before, and he didn't understand why he was noticing now.

"So she wasn't just a missing hiker, was she?" Adriana asked as she walked out of the room. Levi followed her. She was heading for the kitchen and he could hear a coffee maker percolating.

If he drank another cup of coffee he'd probably start to see noises, after all the caffeine he'd had that day already. But if she was making it he wasn't going to turn it down. The machine made noises in the background as the coffee continued brewing.

"I don't think Lara Jones was just a missing hiker." He answered as honestly as he could.

Adriana nodded, then turned away from him. He wished he could see her face to read her facial expressions. He stepped toward her and reached out a hand, though he didn't know why.

She stepped away and opened up a cabinet that was crammed full with coffee mugs stuffed beside each other, on top of each other, as full as it could possibly be without them all falling. "Are you going to tell me more, or did you have questions? I'm not quite sure how this works."

She tossed a glance back at him and Levi just stood there, met her eyes.

Adriana stopped moving. Her eyes widened as their gazes connected and held there, the pull between them almost palpable, at least to Levi.

He swallowed hard.

He didn't even know how to explain what he could feel passing between them. Levi felt more *seen* than he had ever before. It was an awkward, exhilarating closeness they shouldn't have felt because they barely knew each other. But they'd shared so much earlier when she was having her panic attack, and then they'd been shot at...

"Is she why you were shot at?"

Her question confirmed that letting her help him was a good choice. Adriana was smart, observant to the point that he almost wished she'd been a little less good at putting pieces together.

"I believe so." He nodded, still feeling the power of her gaze on his. "Yes."

"You need to let me help you, then." She

said it quietly, then turned away, breaking whatever strange moment had happened between them, when they'd been fully facing each other. She reached for the full coffee carafe, grabbed a mug out of the cabinet and handed it to him. "Coffee?" she asked as she filled two cups.

"Thanks." He accepted the mug the offered and took a sip. Much stronger than he usually made, but this wasn't a woman who did anything halfway or average. Definitely not someone who tended toward "weak" as a word that described either her or her coffee, apparently.

He opened his mouth to continue their conversation and she abruptly moved toward the living room.

"Let's sit."

"Okay." He followed her into the other room, then waited while she sat down. He stayed quiet until she finally looked up at him.

"How are you doing?" He kept his voice calm as he sat. "How are you *really* doing?"

This time, rather than look away, she met his gaze head-on. "I've been better. This afternoon wasn't like me, I hope you know that. I don't usually..." She trailed off.

"I know." And he did. Especially after his relationship with Melissa had fallen apart, Levi knew what it was like to put on an "I'm okay" face for the world. Someone could only keep that up for so long before it cracked.

Especially someone who saw people at their worst like he so often did; she must in her job, also. It was emotionally exhausting, making having a relationship even harder than it was for most people.

He watched Adriana's expression.

She seemed to appreciate his understanding, but something still seemed to be on her mind, so he waited.

"I don't know what else to say," she finally confessed with a shrug that she probably didn't realize was as cute as it was. "I'm embarrassed. But if we are going to be working together, I want to clear the air."

"Are we going to be working together?"

"I would like to."

He still needed to know. So he asked. "But why?"

"Because..." She took a long sip of coffee and turned her head to look out the window. Her gaze was pensive, and then her eyes narrowed. Became more focused.

"What?" He leaned forward, turned to look at whatever she saw.

"Nothing. I... I'm stressed from today is all, I think."

Levi sat back, exhaled. If that was true, he had no business dragging her into this investigation. Today, he feared, was only a glimpse of what the next few weeks or months could hold. If every discovery hit Adriana as hard emotionally as today had, he didn't think he could do that to her. Or her dog, for that matter.

Or himself. Seeing her hurt... It shouldn't affect him so much. They were casual friends at best.

But something about today had made it feel like more than that. Not romantically, though he was undoubtedly attracted to her. But on a deeper level than just friends. Like they knew each other somehow, in a way that mattered.

It would be better for both of them if he'd just ask his questions about the body she'd found and leave. They wouldn't get any closer, there would be no awkwardly charged moments like whatever had happened in the kitchen.

"Adriana..."

Glass from a window shattered on the living-room floor just as he heard the pop of gunfire.

And Adriana fell to the floor.

Two times in one day. She'd been shot at twice in one day.

Adriana was pretty sure she could count this one as being "at" her because it was *her* couch that was likely going to have a hole in it. Or her wall or floor or something. She hadn't seen where the first bullet hit; she'd just fallen to the ground as soon as she heard the glass breaking.

Levi had cried out like she'd been shot and she'd been too frozen to reassure him or say anything until she felt his weight pressing on her, sheltering her, and then she managed to say "I'm okay," though it did nothing to make him move.

She'd shut her dogs in her bedroom before, when she'd heard Levi pull up; that was the one positive aspect of this situation. They were safe.

Herself? She couldn't say the same for sure. More bullets flew, she didn't know how many. The shots were loud, echoing. A rifle, she thought. She'd been around enough of them in her life, when her parents were in the military.

She huddled closer to the couch, desperate for some kind of cover and not sure where to go to find it.

"Can you crawl to the other room if I move?" Levi's voice was breathless. Adriana nodded, then realized he might not be looking at her. He was probably looking out the window. The one she'd said just minutes before didn't have anything interesting out of it. She'd blamed her imagination rather than her senses and it had nearly cost them both their lives.

"Yes," she said, swallowing hard.

"Ready? Go." He lifted himself up and they crawled together for the door to the kitchen. One more shot was fired and Levi heard a lamp fall off the table beside Adriana's couch. He made a note to have the crime-scene team check that spot for bullet casings.

The gunshots stopped. There evidently were no more easily available targets.

Levi was already pulling his phone out of his pocket. She listened as he reported the incident to the police department, his voice out of breath like he'd been running, but not betraying a hint of emotion or terror.

He must feel nothing like she felt. Her heart was fleeing her chest, headed in a dead sprint toward somewhere very far from here and bodies in lakes and bullets and men who were confusing and comforting all at the same time.

Or... She studied him closer. Could it be that having a happy-go-lucky personality was how he dealt with being in situations like this?

She might have misjudged him.

"They'll be here as soon as they can be." He looked to her as soon as he ended the call. "You okay? I'm going to stay in here with you until my team gets here. Tempting as it is to go straight outside and try to see if the shooter is still there, it would be foolish and it would leave you alone. I'm not going to do that."

That he'd ask her that question meant a lot. And further shattered her Levi-doesn't-care-about-anything thoughts. Yes, she'd certainly misjudged him.

Was she okay? That had been his question.

Would she ever be again?

How much could one person take?

She started to cry. *Again.*

"Hey, it's okay."

She braced herself for him to wipe her tears, to tell her to stop. Robert always had done that, and she'd loved him for not wanting her to hurt. It had been sweet.

"Go ahead and cry. It's been an awful day."

Again, this man was not what she expected or understood. He wanted her to cry? She didn't understand, but cry she did, over everything she could think of and none of it all at the same time. She was shaking, her body drained of energy from the shock. Her living room had become a crime scene.

Whoever had been after Levi was after her now, too.

"At this point, I'm...already...involved." She choked the words out between sobs.

"I know." He reached his arms out for her and she didn't protest, but scooted closer on the floor and leaned toward him. He wrapped her upper body in his arms— arms that clearly spent time at the gym or rock climbing, she wasn't sure which— and she felt herself finally relax.

"Thank you," she said to him.

"We really should stop meeting like this,

though," he joked. There was the Levi that drove her crazy when they searched together on occasion. The unflappable guy whose never-takes-things-seriously attitude usually infuriated her.

She knew now, though, that it wasn't that he didn't feel things as deeply or take things as seriously.

It was just that he held things in and dealt with them differently.

Interesting. She wasn't sure how to feel about that.

"What happens now?"

"The department will send guys here to process the scene, check if the shooter's still out there and see if we can gather any evidence or ballistics. They should be able to find the bullets in the living room."

"But it's..." She couldn't make herself say the rest.

"The serial killer. I think so. Or someone he's sent to do his dirty work. It's hard to say." Levi shrugged like he didn't have the weight of the world on his shoulders.

"So if I'm working with you, tell me

what I need to know. About this guy, I mean. What are we dealing with?"

Levi took a deep breath. "Three years ago...well, let me explain. We thought the case started three years ago. I was looking through some cold cases recently and think it may have started before that... But I'll tell you about the recent ones first. Three years ago, a woman disappeared from a coffee shop here in Raven Pass."

"Disappeared? You don't disappear from a restaurant, Levi. Maybe from the woods, or from somewhere isolated, but you don't leave a coffee shop without leaving witnesses to your disappearance."

He shook his head. "I don't know how. I just know it's true. No one in the shop remembers noticing anything out of the ordinary. People saw the victim there, but didn't notice anything else."

She frowned. "Okay, go on."

"She disappeared from a coffee shop. Later she was found dead. A few months later, the same thing—another woman, same coffee shop. Then a similar disappearance from a little coffee place in Gird-wood. Then one at a diner in Hope that served coffee and was the closest thing the town had to a coffee shop."

Adriana was already frowning. "So someone...kills women that were last seen at coffee shops?" She shook her head. Why?

"Serial killers are tricky," he began. "They're not killing in fits of passion or rage, like so many murderers. They're more purposeful and calculated than that. Some of them are trying to right what they believe to be societal wrongs. Some of them are transferring feelings of rage toward someone to other people who look like them. Some of them killed once, maybe even by accident, and now feel compelled to repeat it."

"But Lara Jones wasn't last seen at a coffee shop." Adriana commented.

"No."

"So the killer is changing his MO, or...?"

Levi shook his head. "I'm not jumping to conclusions yet. It's possible that they're shifting a pattern, but this could also just be an outlier. There are other reasons that could explain why the killer deviated from the pattern. They're difficult to figure out or box in."

He shrugged again, but Adriana shuddered.

Whoever was after Levi was a madman, Adriana realized before Levi was even though explaining. The killer's possible motives were nothing short of insanity. Did she want to get involved in such a miry mess?

At the same time, could she do otherwise?

Still, the magnitude of the danger was growing clearer the longer Levi talked. This person had killed multiple times not because he—or she—was angry, but because he believed somehow he was in the right. He'd even tried to kill her and Levi.

Heinous madness.

And Adriana was offering to try to track him down by uncovering his past sins right in front of his eyes, unburying corpses he'd thought were dealt with.

God help me, she prayed, and meant it. Because she felt like she was staring death in the face. And to live, she was going to need help from beyond herself.

FOUR

It didn't take long for Judah to show up. For all their budget woes, Raven Pass PD had excellent response times. Although the fact that it was Judah's younger brother who'd been shot at—twice now today— might account for the speedy arrival. All Levi knew was that within five minutes of calling the station, Judah was banging on Adriana's front door.

"What happened? And what are you mixed up in?"

There was that big-brother tone. Levi shrugged it off with a grin, or at least tried. The truth was it got tiring, having his sibling looking over his shoulder all the time, treating him like, well, a kid.

Maybe it was why he worked so hard,

why he'd felt his whole life like he had something to prove.

"My serial-killer case just heated up," Levi said.

"That's an understatement." Adriana stepped up beside him. "I'm glad the case won't go cold, though. How awful for families, not to have that closure."

It felt nice to have her stand next to him while he talked to his brother.

As much as he wanted this case solved and could see huge value in her helping him find bodies, he didn't want her in danger. If he could go back, not talk to her today at all and keep her safe instead, he would in a heartbeat. No case was worth her safety.

As soon as the thought materialized, it hit him like a punch to the gut, but he shook it away. Of course he wouldn't want her hurt. He would feel that way about any civilian getting involved in a case, right?

Wrong. But he could try to deny that Adriana meant a lot to him for a little longer. Maybe.

But the decision about her being involved or not had been taken out of his hands.

Now what did he do?

"The shots came from where?" Judah looked around for evidence of the attack.

"We were back there in the living room, but they came through the window. So I'd say the backyard," Levi answered. Adriana started that way and Judah followed. Levi brought up the rear, trying to work out the best way out of this situation he'd unwittingly placed Adriana in.

"We were sitting here." She was already giving him a walk-through, back in that room, and still she seemed unshakable. How was she the same woman who'd broken down today over a body? Levi wasn't minimizing the value of life, but he did wonder how she could be so strong most of the time and then just...break like she had today.

And she hadn't seemed surprised at her outburst, really, just embarrassed that he had been there to see it.

"...then the shots." Adriana finished what she'd been saying and Levi focused back in, realizing he'd missed part of that conversation.

"Did you tell Judah you thought you saw something out the window before the shooting began?" he asked.

She raised an eyebrow. "Of course. Not paying attention?"

Okay, yeah, she didn't appreciate that. He got it.

"She did," Judah answered, "and she also mentioned something about helping you on your case?"

His brother's tone left no question about what he thought about that idea.

"I told you, I offered. Insisted, actually."

"That may be a plan you want to rethink." Judah started out looking at Adriana, but it was Levi's gaze he held as he finished his statement. More like a command.

"It's not like I'm safe if I'm not involved, am I, Officer Wicks?" Adriana asked Judah. She'd folded her arms over her chest, almost like she didn't appreciate Judah blaming Levi for both shootings.

But she met his gaze and again, he felt like she understood his complicated relationship with his brother.

Levi looked away. It was starting to be disconcerting to be read so well. And how did she do that, anyway? A woman who spent more time with her dogs on her days off than other people, if rumors could be trusted.

"I can see your point," Judah finally conceded, his voice rough. "Levi, is this something you've run past the chief?"

A question he would have preferred to discuss *not* in front of Adriana, but sure, why wouldn't they talk about that now, too.

"I need to run it past him."

He braced for Adriana's judgmental look, but nothing. Just a small nod.

"Do that." Judah's gaze swung between the two of them. "I'm not sure I think it's a good idea, but…" Levi opened his mouth. Judah held out a hand. "It's not my choice,

Levi. I get it." Another look at Adriana. "But if I were you I'd think extremely hard before I started literally digging up the past. It might help with this case, but is it going to hurt you?"

"That's not the question here." Adriana's tone was still pleasant enough, but her shoulders were tense. "And someone's already tried to hurt me."

Judah nodded. "All right, I'll process the scene and ballistics here, see if I can get any clearer of a picture of where the shooter might have been. There are a couple of officers outside." He motioned out the window. "And we'll try to pinpoint where he or she was in case we can get any forensic evidence from whatever was essentially a sniper's perch."

"I'll come with you." Levi was ready to keep working on this. "If you're okay here?"

Adriana nodded. He should have known she would be. Part of him wanted to stay and talk to her more, but frankly, at the moment he was too off balance. He needed space and not to feel helpless. This was the closest he'd ever been to being the victim of any kind of crime and it had happened twice in one day. It was unacceptable and working was the only way he knew to deal with it.

He followed Judah back down the hall toward Adriana's front door, promising himself he'd check in with Adriana later, as well as make sure someone sat in her driveway in a patrol car that night. He'd do it himself, but that would probably just attract more trouble since he was the main target.

"You're sure about this?" Judah asked when they were outside.

"Helping with the case?" Levi shrugged. "I don't think it's a conflict of interest. If we left a case every time someone tried to intimidate us, we wouldn't get a lot done, would we?"

"You know that's not what I mean." Judah was walking toward the woods behind Adriana's house. It was mostly spruce trees, with some hardwoods, too.

Full, leafed out from summer, but the leaves were changing now in the middle of September, starting to fall down.

"Adriana is an adult, Judah. And she's the best cadaver-dog handler in the area, maybe the state. I've talked to people, asked for recommendations in case I ever had the money to hire someone to help on a contract basis, and it's her name that comes up, even as far away as Anchorage."

"She looks at you like it's morning and you're a hot cup of coffee."

"That is the strangest thing I've ever heard you say." Levi shook his head, feeling a rush of heat come to his cheeks. Why would how she looked at him affect him at all? She was helping him with a case. That was all. If she was prettier than any of the partners he usually had, smarter, more intriguing, none of that mattered, right? "Not only does she look at me completely normally, but that's just a weird expression."

"Think what you want. She doesn't look at you the same way she looks at me."

Snarky comments hovered on the tip of his tongue. Saying them would be admitting that Judah was right, and while Levi didn't know how Adriana looked at him, he didn't think it was like his brother said.

Actually, he desperately hoped it wasn't. Because as much as he'd felt *something* between them today—the flickers of something, anyway—Levi wasn't the kind of guy who was going to settle down. No, he had tried that once and it had gone wrong. All wrong and it had been all his fault.

At least Judah hadn't brought that up. His brother must have understood that some wounds went too deep to be thrown into someone's face so casually.

Together they walked into the woods and the general area from where the shots had come as they searched for evidence. Levi glanced back at Adriana's town house. The angle was wrong from here, but the distance might not be.

"How did the shots have any chance of

hitting us, fired from an upward angle like this?" Levi asked his brother.

"You don't think someone was set up in a tree?" The tall spruce trees were high enough to be a possibility, but they were thin trunked and not something a person could put a deer stand in.

"Here," Judah called a minute later. The grass underneath one spruce tree had been tamped down, like someone had been lying on it.

Levi frowned. Not what he'd been expecting at all. He turned around.

The view into the room from there was good enough. Adriana's oversized windows that went almost to the floor had provided the shooter with enough of a vantage point to be able to tell when they were there and when they'd crawled to another room.

But the angle of the shots would have made it difficult for the shooter to hit them. It wasn't an impossible trajectory, and they'd still been in real danger, but it was strange. Had whoever fired the shots been unable to set up in a more viable sniper's perch? Or had the shots only been intended to scare them?

Did that change how they investigated?

"Someone was rushed," Judah said when he walked over.

Levi nodded his agreement. For all the tension between them, Levi knew his brother was a smart guy, a good cop. It was why Levi had followed him here to Raven Pass after his life in Anchorage had blown up in his face.

Literally.

"So whoever is after me isn't a professional killer or a hit man..." Levi said slowly.

Judah's expression said that he agreed. "No..."

Levi suggested, "It's the serial killer himself."

The officers working to process the scene had told Adriana that her leaving the house wasn't necessary, but asked that she stay out of the living room while they processed. So she went to the kitchen and started cooking dinner.

She had friends who would argue that if ever there was a night for takeout, the day you'd been shot at more than once was it. But cooking had always helped Adriana calm down, even from the time she was a little girl. There was something about having her hands busy, about seeing all the ingredients come together to make a meal, feeding not just herself but other people. All of it gave her life and helped her cope when…

Well, everything had fallen apart. Again.

Adriana reached into the fridge, grabbed an onion and set it down on the cutting board she'd already placed on the counter. She took a knife from the knife block and started the reassuringly monotonous chopping process as her mind ran through the day.

Their missing hiker was dead. She assumed the cops always got called when bodies were unearthed, but she also assumed there was evidence that the death had not been accidental.

Chop, chop, chop.

She'd been shot at in her house. Her living-room window was in shards on her nice floor.

Chop, chop.

Most unbelievably, she'd broken down in front of Levi. Cried. Had a full-blown panic attack.

Chop, chop, chop, chop, chop.

Adriana blinked moisture out of the corners of her eyes and blamed it on the onion. Never mind that it was a Vidalia sweet onion.

Having finished chopping, she continued pulling ingredients from the fridge. Spinach. Ricotta cheese. Pasta shells from the pantry.

A day like today called for carbs and cheese. Adriana had never been one of those women whose goal was to be thin. She just wanted to be fit enough to do her job well and enjoy Alaska.

She put the pasta on to boil and wondered for half a crazy second if Levi would stay for dinner if she asked. It wasn't that...

Well, she knew better than to let herself feel...

She didn't like him like that!

Adriana dumped the spinach in a bowl and slammed the cabinet shut behind her.

He'd been patient and understanding today; that was why her mind was all weird and confused. He'd been a decent human and he hadn't made fun of her little breakdown. She'd been feeling the same about...

Well, no, she couldn't imagine having this kind of...pull toward Judah even if he'd been in the same situation.

She couldn't have a crush on Levi. Could it even be called a crush when both people were adults and should be above such things as "listen to your heart" or "follow your feelings"?

Or when falling in love wasn't an option for her?

Adriana had let it happen once, and her

heart had been crushed so badly it had only just started to heal. Or at least she'd assumed that it had until today, when she'd been crouched on the cold dirt next to a man she only knew in a professional capacity, trying to remind herself how to breathe.

She couldn't afford to let that happen to her again. She'd seen what love could do to people when she was growing up. She didn't want to be that way. She had goals, dreams.

A solid determination to be better than previous generations of her family.

She wouldn't invite him for dinner, wouldn't let him get any closer to her.

Would. Not. Be. Like. Her. Mother.

Levi walked in. "Wow, something smells good."

She had just put the now-stuffed shells into the oven. "It's dinner…" She turned and her eyes caught his.

"Want to stay and eat with me? I made too much for one, anyway." Was that really her voice, her traitorous voice?

He didn't answer right away. She felt every kind of stupid. Her cheeks heated and she looked away from him.

"I'd love to stay."

Oh.

Well.

"All right." She nodded, pulled two plates from the cabinet and busied herself setting the table in her adjoining dining nook.

"Do you want to know? What we found out in the woods, I mean?"

If she ignored him, would he go away? Or at least not follow her to the table but give her a minute to collect her thoughts? She was used to being competent, maybe even a bit intimidating to people.

She still was, according to her search-and-rescue team. Apparently it was just this...weirdness of today that was turning her this way.

Some help here would be great, God. Praying hadn't occurred to her earlier, which she felt bad about. There had been a time in her life when it was the first thing she did in any situation that made her uncomfortable, but Robert's death had changed that. She and God...well, it wasn't that they had a bad relationship, but Adriana just didn't quite trust Him like she had before. He'd let her down, hadn't He? Not come through when she'd needed Him to.

"You can tell me if you are allowed," Adriana finally answered, glancing over at him. His expression looked relieved. That was one thing she appreciated about Levi—at least he wasn't difficult to read.

"We found the place where he had been sitting. Not sure what significance it has yet, and we didn't find any solid forensic evidence so far. But there are still officers out looking it over. If there is something to be found, they will find it."

Adriana nodded. "Good."

Levi grabbed the silverware she'd set on the table and while she was setting out napkins, he started to put it down.

"The woman you found in the lake today?" he said as he did the chore, not looking at her. Something in his voice warned her that they were still talking about the case.

"Yes?" She did her best to brace herself even though she felt her chest tighten, her breathing become more shallow, as she imagined the scene.

"I believe she's tied to my case because her hands were zip-tied, Adriana. She didn't drown, not on accident the way..." He trailed off but she knew what he meant and heard every single word that he was merciful enough not to say.

Did that make her feel better? She didn't know. A life had still been lost, wasted. And zip-tied...

A life had been stolen, as she'd suspected and he'd hinted at earlier, the way he'd implied that the serial killer had something to do with her missing—now murdered, it turned out—hiker case.

"So this is for sure tied to your case," she clarified.

"I'm almost certain."

"How do you want to start the search?"

she asked him, finally daring to meet his gaze. He shook his head, regret lining his features.

"Let's talk after dinner. We both need a break."

He'd been the one to start the discussion, did he realize that? Adriana wanted to point that out to him, but it didn't seem polite. Instead she just nodded and brought dinner to the table.

They sat to eat and as Levi prayed over their food, Adriana felt herself wondering what the next few days—make that even just the next few hours—were going to hold.

The gunshots confirmed they were making progress on the case. If they weren't, then whoever was behind all this wouldn't take the risk to attack them, possibly being caught in the process. It spoke of a criminal who was desperate.

But desperate criminals were often the most dangerous. And Adriana knew she and Levi were the ones in the crosshairs.

FIVE

Levi had barely been able to focus during dinner.

He had so much he wanted to talk about, details of the case he'd gotten permission to share.

But she'd been starting to look pale when she was setting the table and he'd been concerned they were going to have a repeat of this morning.

So he'd told her they'd talk about it after dinner. And he'd spent the entirety of the meal making plans, thinking of areas they should search, information he should give her.

He tried to keep up a polite conversation with her, said goodbye to the officers who were processing the living room once they'd finished, and headed out. But as he did all that, he was debating what he was about to do—and asking himself how much he should tell Adriana. How much she needed to know.

She'd seemed relatively unaware of his internal struggle. Her color had turned back to normal and he was feeling fairly confident now that she wasn't going to...

What, fall apart again? Levi was sure Adriana wouldn't appreciate even being thought of in the terms he'd been pondering.

"So what were you thinking? " she asked him once she returned from clearing their plates and going to let her dogs out. She'd kept them locked up while the officers were processing the scene. He'd started to stand up to help with the dishes but she had waved him off.

"Thinking about what?" he asked as she sat back down.

"The..." She took a breath. "The murders. The investigation. Where do we start?"

"You really don't have to do this." The words came out before he could take them back, charging ahead without his permission. He couldn't afford not to have her help, so he wished he could yank back the offer, hold her to her promise.

But when he looked at her, her eyes were shooting sparks and it appeared he didn't need to backpedal. She was going to help, anyway. Regardless of how much it cost her emotionally.

"You aren't seriously trying to get rid of me already, are you?" She met his gaze head-on, immovable in front of him.

"I can't..." He trailed off and then decided honesty was always the best policy, but especially with Adriana. "Listen, are you sure about this?"

"How many times do we need to have this conversation?"

"I know, but—"

"Earlier. You doubt that I can handle it because of earlier, right? Is that how it's going to be, Levi? One mistake, one time that I accidentally break down..."

She stood up and walked to the coffee maker.

"Adriana…" He started to talk but she pressed the coffee grinder.

Kind of hard to talk over that.

He waited.

She turned to him when it was done. "Listen, the way I see it we have two choices. One, I can help you, and you can treat me like a functioning adult who is doing you a favor and is capable and strong. That panic attack was an *exception*." She emphasized the word, but her facial expression wavered. Was she doubting herself? Was that why she was coming down so hard on him? "Or," she continued, "we can forget it. I'll try to stay safe, you can try to solve the case without critical evidence. But I will not tolerate being treated like a child in any way."

He was pretty sure that she'd have walked out by now if it wasn't her town house.

Levi nodded. "I'm sorry. I didn't mean to make you feel that way."

She eyed him, finished making the coffee without a word and then set the two mugs down on the table.

"So...coffee?"

He nodded.

She got the carafe, poured out the coffee, then sat. "What's the plan?"

"I don't think we should try to do much tonight." This wasn't his usual way of doing things—telling people to take some time, to rest. When he was on a case, he was driven. Focused. Determined. And that had helped him in the past. Professionally, anyway.

Personally...

It had been what his ex-wife had blamed all their struggles on.

He couldn't be trying to correct for that now, right? What did it matter if Adriana thought he was hyperfocused? He wasn't trying to start any kind of relationship with her. And besides, she'd made it clear more than once that she didn't have regard for his focus at all. Actually, she'd looked at him judgmentally before when he'd tried to affect a laid-back attitude.

She let cases affect her personally. That much was obvious after today. He couldn't do that, not the way she did, and expect to keep doing this job. He needed to have some emotional distance.

"Okay." She just nodded, not seeming to mind either way.

Levi didn't comment. No need to stir anything up if they were both happy.

"So I should probably let you get home, then, huh?" Adriana took a sip of her coffee and then stood, moving back toward her coffee area. "I've got a to-go cup here somewhere."

Levi stayed quiet again. That hadn't been what he was going for, but if she didn't want him here...

He stood up. "I'll head home. You're okay here on your own?"

She nodded.

Should he tell her that he'd already talked to Judah, who had promised he'd stay in the driveway in a patrol car that night? It would be foolish for Levi to sit on her house when he had a target on his back.

But there wasn't any chance he was leaving her unprotected.

Finally, honesty won out. Adriana wouldn't appreciate things being kept from her. And on a practical level, she was likely to notice a car in her driveway. Might as well explain now.

"An officer will be in your driveway all night, keeping an eye on things. You should be safe."

It was that *should be* that was going to make it hard for him to sleep. If he knew her better, he might ask to crash on her couch downstairs, just to reassure himself. At the moment, though, it made more sense to let his brother handle it. He'd have to just trust someone else to keep an eye on her.

She met his gaze then, but rather than argue, she just nodded. Her expression softened, ever so slightly, and he wondered if she was regretting essentially kicking him out.

"So we're good?" she asked as she handed him the coffee.

It was probably as close to an apology for the brush-off that he was going to get. And that was fine. He didn't deserve one, really. He just couldn't help that the way she'd clammed up on him and asked him to leave had hurt his feelings some.

He nodded. "We're good."

He took the coffee from her and headed to his car, waving to Judah as he climbed into his cruiser.

Tomorrow they'd compile a list of women who'd gone missing between the first wave of serial-killer cases and the second. There had been some talk at the time of whether or not those disappearances could have been linked to the serial killer, but nothing conclusively linked them. In Alaska, people went missing often, sometimes from trips into the wilderness gone wrong, with no foul play.

With the help of Adriana and her dog, they might be able to find a lead there.

The possibilities were bright enough that he almost didn't want to go to sleep. But if he didn't, he wouldn't be able to give his best to this case.

And he needed to give it his best or Adriana would be in danger.

And that was unacceptable.

Darkness hadn't fully come until Levi left, well after dinner. Adriana always appreciated that even though darkness had finally come to Alaska at night after several months of mostly daylight, they still had more daylight than many other parts of the country in mid-September.

Now, though, it was after ten and she was trying to go to sleep. The darkness outside was heavy. Inky-black and suffocating.

But not suffocating the fear that had come when night had fallen.

Adriana always slept with her blinds open and had crawled in bed with them that way tonight. Now, having tried to sleep for a long half hour, she stood up, walked to the window and pulled them down.

Having an officer in her driveway reassured her somewhat.

But...what if the shooter was still out there?

Murder was difficult enough to imagine. But the concept of a serial killer, someone who committed a crime over and over...

She shuddered and returned to bed. Tried to pull the covers up higher, but Blue and Babe were lying on them. She patted the spot next to her and the dogs moved closer, giving her a chance to yank at the covers.

She relaxed a little, her pets having moved closer. But her eyes kept drifting to the window. How could someone commit crimes like this? And how could she have gotten involved?

It was one thing to try to get some kind of closure to families. Another to help bring a serial killer to justice.

She wasn't ready for this.

Or was she?

Of course, she thought as she rolled over, giving up would prove that Levi had been right to doubt her. It would be succumbing to fear.

And Adriana didn't do that.

Ever.

She sighed. Turned over again. And prayed morning would come quickly, and with it, some kind of resolution that would make this case easy to solve.

She wanted to be free from this fear. And the only way to do that was to figure out who was behind these murders and put them in prison.

By the time morning finally came, Adriana had managed to sleep some. She hesitantly walked down the stairs, let her dogs into the backyard to do their morning business and then went back inside to make coffee.

Her unease from the night before had been partially chased away by the light, but only partially. They'd been shot at it in broad daylight twice yesterday.

Her cell phone beeped a text-message alert as she sipped her coffee.

In your driveway now. Let me know when you're awake and ready—Levi

She glanced down at her sweatpants and sweatshirt.

No point in pretending she was the kind of girl who woke up looking like she'd stepped out of some kind of fashion magazine.

I've got coffee on if you want it, she texted back and waited. Five minutes later he was knocking on the door.

"Ready for today?"

"As I can be." She hoped her smile made up for the uncertainty of her words. "What's the plan?"

"How about we talk about it while we drink that coffee you mentioned? I ran out of the house this morning so I'd appreciate it."

"Sure." Was it her imagination or was her heart beating a little faster than it should have been?

She walked to the coffee maker and poured him a cup, her mind racing as she tried to imagine what today was going to look like. She'd already talked to Blue about the day; while some people would probably think it was strange to talk to a dog, Blue was her partner. Besides, she had read some study saying dogs knew thousands of words.

"I thought we'd start off by going to some of the burial sites to see if there's further evidence buried there that we missed and see if we can find anything else…with your dog." He added the last part like it was necessary. Adriana knew her K9 was the valuable one here and it made her laugh. Levi's face turned red. A man who blushed. Interesting. She didn't mind that at all.

Clearly he felt things much more deeply than she'd ever thought he did.

"I didn't mean you aren't a necessary part of the search..."

As well trained as Blue was, she worked with Adriana, who, as her handler, was the one with the skills to assess her cues and make human judgment calls on what they might mean. It was part of why she'd been drawn to dog handling when she'd decided to get involved in SAR work after Robert's death. She figured that being able to help people—and to do that with animals she loved—would bring her closure. Adriana might not be as cute as her dog, but she was essential to the team. She knew it well enough not to need the reassurance, though the way he was stumbling over himself was sort of cute.

"Relax, Levi. You're fine." She sat back down and took a sip of her coffee. "Do you have any more plans for finding them? Like, any kind of system for how to canvass those areas?"

He shook his head and had the good grace to look a little embarrassed. She appreciated that. He wasn't running the search the way she would and it was nice that he knew that.

"So rather than do that..." She wasn't sure how he'd react to her idea, but she'd thought about it last night and the idea wouldn't go away, so it might be one that was worth considering. "What if we plotted out where you've found all the bodies so far? See what I mean? Like a map that shows the killer's preferred burial locations—they were all buried, right?" She realized she wasn't sure.

He nodded, confirming her assumption. Other than the one they'd found yesterday in the lake. She wondered what it could mean, that the killer had started deviating from his pattern of burying his victims, or that something had been different about this murder.

"So if they're all buried, besides that one, and you said not to draw conclusions from one outlier," she continued, doing her best not to let her mind settle on the memories of the empty expanse of lake and a water-logged body, "then I think it would be useful to see them on a map. The killer must have had some kind of pattern, right?"

Levi seemed to consider it for a minute. "I can see what you're saying. It's different from our usual approach." He was frowning now, his eyebrows pulled together, maybe in concentration, maybe in frustration. Adriana didn't know him well enough to be able to tell.

"Is it worth it, though?" she asked it in a soft voice as she took another sip of coffee, and he nodded almost immediately.

"Yes." Levi kept nodding. "Yes, I think it is." He set down his coffee mug. "Okay, do you have a piece of paper? I like to visualize things."

Adriana reached for her iPad, which was sitting on the counter, and handed it to him. It was open to one of her favorite drawing-and-plotting apps.

He raised his eyebrows. "Do you have any of the old-fashioned kind of paper that comes with a pencil?"

She smirked. Handed him the white Apple Pencil.

He shook his head. "Okay..." His fingers looked adorably clumsy—she noticed without wanting to. The adorable part, anyway. Finally, she laughed, stood, walked to one of her kitchen drawers and pulled out a yellow legal pad and an actual pencil.

"Thanks." He laughed. "We aren't exactly that tech friendly at Raven Pass PD, so my tech skills are behind."

"We use it when it's useful." Adriana shrugged. "Sometimes it's not and the old-fashioned way is better, but I do like having it."

"I'll take a legal pad any day."

"There's probably an app for that." She laughed.

Levi started sketching out a rough map: just the main road into Raven Pass, some general areas, like parks, shops, trailheads and hiking trails. "It's not superdetailed," he explained, "but I think it'll give us a start, anyway, to see if there are any obvious clusters, features, things like that."

"Features?" She knew the word, clearly, but wasn't sure what he meant in that context.

"Like sometimes killers will bury bodies next to water, or by a certain kind of tree—things like that can be part of a signature or MO."

Adriana nodded. She hadn't known that. "Makes sense. So where were the bodies?"

"Here…" He marked one *X*. Then another. "Here… Here."

"Okay, and the women who disappeared and whose bodies were not found? The ones you suspect could be tied to the case but aren't sure about? Those women went missing in between the first killing spree and this most recent one, right?"

Levi nodded. "I have those details back at the police department." He glanced down at her sweatpants. Adriana looked at him, a smile tugging at the corners of her face as she waited for his comment.

"Are you, uh, ready to go?"

Bless his heart. He was trying so hard not to ask the obvious question, which was "Are you wearing that?" Half of her wondered if he'd grown up with sisters to know that such a question wasn't a good idea, or if he was just an extraordinarily smart man.

"I do have to go change first," she told him, letting a small smile creep up.

He laughed. Not a small laugh, but a full-out loud one, like he was zero percent ashamed of his humor.

"Sorry," he said again, but unlike earlier, he didn't seem sorry. Actually, since she'd suggested different search techniques, the mood between them had shifted. Like he was finally comfortable working with her, like they might be part of a team.

Huh.

She was already part of the search-and-rescue team, but it was different than this, the respect she saw in his eyes now.

Why did Levi's opinion matter so much?

"I'll be back in a minute." She took a

long, last sip of coffee and hurried up the stairs, without waiting to hear what else Levi had to say.

Suddenly the idea of spending all day today with him, not to mention the many more days it would take for them to solve this case, seemed overwhelming. How was she supposed to keep a grip on these feelings, whatever they were, when they were in such close proximity so often?

She wasn't sorry she'd volunteered, though. Adriana needed to remember that, and no matter how distracting Levi was, she needed to keep her eyes focused on what they were doing.

Stopping the killer before anyone else became the next victim. Getting a criminal behind bars.

Making their world safe again.

Yes, that should be enough to keep her focused. Even with a distractingly handsome officer on the case with her.

SIX

Sitting in Adriana's kitchen drinking coffee she'd made was a little surreal, since up until yesterday they'd had very few conversations with each other. It had always seemed like she'd avoided talking to him.

All he knew was that he liked how things were now and he had no desire to go back to the strained relationship they'd had before.

Interesting.

He took another sip of coffee. His phone beeped and he pulled it out to check it.

Jim, his old partner.

Heard you had some excitement yesterday. Everything all right?

What did he want to say to him? Levi respected the years the man had put into the case, but Jim wasn't an officer anymore and it wasn't appropriate to discuss it the same way he would have in the past.

Maybe that was the wrong way to think of it. Levi was still stinging from yesterday's close call, and the fewer people who knew about the situation, the better.

It was strange, counting his old partner as one of the people he couldn't talk to, though.

And probably an overreaction. But, Levi justified, part of why Jim had retired had been to spend more time with family. He knew from the man's vague comments that he and his wife of something like forty years had been through some rough patches. Likely due to the stress that police officers' jobs put on their marriages.

Everything's okay. Gotta have excitement now and then to have a job and some of us can't afford to retire yet.

Levi sent the message and smiled to himself. Jim's dry sense of humor had rubbed off, which was just fine with him. It was standard police-officer humor.

His brother's face then came to mind. Half the time he wasn't sure Judah *had* a sense of humor.

Or it might just be that Judah was still hurting from the rough time he'd gone through years ago, when his fiancée had died. Part of him thought he should ask about that, but lately he didn't feel like he knew his brother well enough to know what would help him or how he'd respond to things.

No, better to let it go. Continue with this weirdly cordial relationship they'd had since Levi moved up here. Levi sure didn't want Judah prying into his past relationship with his ex-wife, so maybe Levi owed it to him to let him grieve in peace, if that was what had caused his moodiness lately.

"I'm ready." Adriana took the last few

steps quickly and then skidded a little in her socked feet on the hard floor.

Her dark hair swung as she skidded and her arms flailed out to catch herself, and then she turned to him with a grin.

He had to muffle another smile. He did that a lot with her, he was noticing. Funny, for someone who'd accused him of being too lighthearted about his work, she was pretty funny and easygoing herself.

He took that thought back just over an hour later. They'd loaded into his car—him, Adriana and her dog Blue—and started for his office. There they'd picked up his files and case notes, and then they'd headed to the location where the first body of the most recent string of murders had been found. If Levi was correct, that would make it the fourth body out of eight. Three from the first string of killings, four from the more recent and now Lara Jones. Not to mention the gap in time where Levi was still wondering if more women could have been killed whose bodies just hadn't been discovered. He had told Adriana not to jump to conclusions about the burial location changing with Lara Jones. But if they found another body that hadn't been buried, that would change.

On the other hand, if all the other bodies they found had been buried, then they'd know this hiker's burial had been an exception for some reason. Something nagged Levi's brain about that, told him that this exception could tell him something about the case, but he didn't know what yet. They were nearing the parking lot for a trailhead when Adriana, who'd been quiet since they left the police department, spoke.

"So this was the first murder?" Adriana frowned, like she was trying to put it all together.

"I worked on a set of serial-killer cases that started with this one. Of those, yes, it's the first. But two days ago, in the cold-case room, I found several old cases, from more than two decades back, that look extremely similar to the cases I've been working. There were three of those. If this one is related, it would be the fourth chronologically. That we know of."

"So you think the same killer was killing years before you were on the case or started working here?"

Levi nodded. "Yes, but somehow they hadn't been connected before."

Her frown deepened and this time it was less concentration and more judgment. "How did someone not notice that?"

He shrugged. "You have to understand, cases have many pieces, important details, so it's easy to overlook connections if you don't have a reason to suspect any. In this instance, no one who was at the department back then is still at the department. So no one made the connection and the boxes sat in the cold-case room."

"Until you did."

He nodded.

"Then you found them and then got shot at." She frowned. "And then..."

He could see the wheels in her head turning. Yes, then she'd discovered the missing hiker at the bottom of a lake, and the woman's hands had been tied in a way reminiscent of his serial-killer case.

"My missing hiker."

He didn't like the way she used personal pronouns and took ownership of her search. No wonder she carried the toll so heavily if she took every single loss personally, like she was losing someone she cared about again. He understood it might be some kind of PTSD related to her loss of Robert, but he still wondered if it was the healthiest way to deal with it. He'd found in his line of work that you had to be able to step back emotionally to survive. It didn't mean you cared about people less. It just meant that you knew that separating yourself was sometimes necessary in order to help others.

"You mentioned her hands were zip-tied," Adriana said with too much calm in her voice. Levi felt his shoulders tense as he watched her grip on the handle on the side of his car tighten. He'd agonized over how much information to give her, but she had insisted she could handle it and she was an adult.

"Yes."

Her eyebrows pulled together. "Definitely not typical. So your thought is..." She waited for him to explain.

Levi opened his mouth to explain that it was too soon to draw conclusions when his mind finally landed on the implication that had been nagging at him.

He'd been right to tell her that the killer's MO hadn't necessarily changed. When multiple bodies had been discovered buried and only one in a lake, it didn't make sense to assume everything about the pattern had changed.

Which should make him ask the question—why had this hiker been found in a lake? Why hadn't she been last seen at a coffee shop?

The answer hit him with the force of a slap.

Because Lara Jones hadn't been one of the killer's intended victims.

"I think," he continued as his mind kept

working out its conclusions, "that while Lara Jones was hiking she found something she shouldn't have, like another body or the burial of one. Either would fit. And to keep her quiet, after zip-tying her to stop her from leaving, the serial killer murdered her also. But disposed of her in a lake because it was convenient and she wasn't one of his or her typical victims, so the MO mattered less."

He waited for her to comment, but she said nothing. He pulled the car into the trailhead parking lot and drove into a spot, noting that the lot was fairly empty, which made sense for a weekday. Searching here made less sense to him now that he'd had his realization about Lara Jones, but he needed more information from Adriana first before he figured out their next move.

"Where was her car found?" he asked.

"The Evergreen Point trails. Near the lake."

Close enough that there were trails where someone could dump a body into the lake without ever being seen.

There. That was where they needed to start. He was sure of it.

"Do you mind if we come back to this search?" Levi asked her, not waiting for an answer before he put the car back in Drive.

"You don't want to search around here first and see if the killer hid more bodies near the first you found?"

There she was, frowning again. She did that a lot when she was thinking, he'd noticed, which explained why he'd assumed their personalities were completely different. It turned out that was her thinking face.

Seemed like maybe she wasn't the only one who had made incorrect assumptions about someone. He was guilty of that, too.

"Oh…" Her voice trailed off and she looked up at him. "You think there is a new body, a new death in this latest round of serial-killer cases. And that Lara Jones discovered the body."

Her voice was grave, her face utterly

expressionless in a way Levi would have thought wasn't possible.

"And then was killed because of it. Making her not an intended victim that would fit the killer's MO, but just someone who was in the wrong place at the wrong time and needed to be silenced." He nodded as he spoke.

Adriana's eyes were wide. "Go. We need to find out."

She felt it, too—the need to give people closure, to stay on top of things.

And talking things out with her had helped clarify the case in his mind, helped him piece things together. If they were going to work together, he needed to keep reminding himself that she was in this just as much as he was. *Trust her. Work with her like a real partner.*

But he would also try to remind himself that this was only for one case; that soon enough he'd be on his own again and she'd be back to rescuing the living.

* * *

Everything made sense, now that Adriana had all the pieces.

Levi had a case involving a serial killer. He discovered similarities to a cold case. He hurried to the lake when the strangeness of the missing hiker being zip-tied had been discovered, or in any case he'd discovered that soon after he got there.

The killer, then, must have been watching. Even before he—or she—had shot at them, Adriana realized with a force that made it hard to swallow. How close had they been?

Since the shots had missed, it couldn't have been too close.

Could it have been?

Unless the shots were meant to warn.

For a minute, Adriana wanted to call this all off. She stared out the window, wondered what her team was doing today and if they needed her. Levi had texted last night and told her that he'd talked to her team leader, Jake Stone, about her taking a break from her search-and-rescue duties to work as a contractor for the police department. She had some vacation time saved up so she'd be able to take it for a couple of weeks, and if she needed to work after that ran out, her savings account was healthy enough that she could take a small hit financially.

She felt like she was doing the right thing. But this was hard, looking for bodies someone had left on purpose. Before now, she would have said she'd seen the heaviest things life had to offer, what with all the searches she'd done that hadn't ended well. Alaska was a harsh place, where the line between adventure and irresponsible risk was as thin as a razor's edge.

But the people she and her team had found dead in Alaska hadn't been killed maliciously. Their lives had been seemingly stolen, but not literally. They had just...died. Risked too much, gone too far.

These people she was looking for now had been murdered, in cold blood.

The difference was huge.

She scratched Blue behind her soft white ears. The dog looked into her eyes and Adriana would have sworn Blue could read her thoughts.

How would this different kind of search affect her K9 partner? Would it be too much for the sensitive Alaskan husky she'd come to love so much?

Adriana hoped not.

She exhaled deeply.

She couldn't quit, though. Not knowing that her work could help end this sooner and save someone's life before it was threatened.

She'd gotten into search-and-rescue work in the first place to save people like Robert—people who had accidents in the backcountry and needed to be rescued. Even though working with Levi wasn't quite the same, it fulfilled the same kind of catharsis she was looking for.

She hadn't been able to save the man she loved. But there were people she could save.

Starting now. Lives might depend on her involvement.

Because the killer would keep killing. There was no doubt about that, after what Levi had told her this morning.

"Adriana."

She looked up, realized the landscape outside the car window was no longer moving, but was still. They were here.

"Sorry. I was..." What could she say? Distracted? Preoccupied?

Terrified about what she'd gotten herself into, yet somehow eager to get started so it would all be over?

"I was thinking," she said as she swallowed hard. This was enough, this living with her emotions so very close to the surface. There was a job to do, and it was time to go into work mode and focus in.

Lives were at stake.

She sat up a little straighter, then petted Blue behind her ears, something that had always seemed to calm both of them down.

"The Forest Lake system has more than twenty miles of trails," he told her. Adriana had already known that—she'd searched this area a few years back after a little kid had gotten separated from his mom while hiking. The child had been found within an hour or so of the SAR team being called, thanks to her dog catching the scent.

The feeling of satisfaction and victory from that would help her now; at least she hoped so.

"So do you want to start here at the entrance?"

"Let's get into the woods a bit, where the scent would be more preserved," she suggested.

She walked into the woods, and when she was sure no one else was around, she let Blue off her leash. The dog trotted ahead of her, her body language relaxed, her eyes focused. She was keeping alert, Adriana could tell.

"Can you talk while she works, or is that against some kind of code?" Levi asked from where he hiked beside her, matching her pace close to perfectly.

"I can talk." Adriana glanced at him,

seeing that he was smiling slightly. She turned her eyes back to Blue. "I just have to watch her in case she alerts."

"How does she do that?"

His voice sounded genuinely curious, with none of the skepticism she'd heard in the tones of some people.

"Technically she's trained for a bark alert, since she's an air-scent dog and works off-leash," Adriana explained, glancing at Levi now and then to make sure he was really interested. He still seemed like it. "But sometimes I notice her body language before she actually barks."

"She stays pretty close to you, then?"

"Blue does. That's not necessarily typical of air-scent dogs. Some of them will run a good bit away, then alert, and the handler has to chase them down." She laughed. "Blue likes to keep me where she can see me."

"Even when she finds a scent?"

Adriana nodded. "She'll typically stay within sight of me no matter what. I guess she figures the scent will still be there, even if she waits for me."

He nodded and they kept walking. Adriana figured he must be tired of making conversation when he was working, which she understood. She hoped he didn't feel like he had to talk to her. Sometimes walking through the woods with someone else with no conversation was actually welcome.

"What made you decide to become an SAR handler?" Levi asked.

The man was more of an extroverted conversationalist than she was. It was kind of nice, though. With so many people she knew, she was the one who kept the conversation going. She felt the opposite with Levi, and it was a welcome change.

"I didn't even know it was a job until I was halfway through college."

Had she meant to admit that? She hadn't really stopped to think before she spoke, a fault of hers for most of her life.

Even her search-and-rescue team didn't know this part of her story. They just knew that she came highly recommended from the SAR training team in Anchorage, where she'd learned her trade after Robert's accident.

They didn't know about the accident, either. And Levi did.

He might as well know everything.

"I went to college in Oklahoma, where I'm from. When I lived there I met this guy who was from Alaska. We fell in love, got engaged, and when he wanted to go back to Alaska, I went with him. I'd have followed him anywhere."

She stopped talking.

"Adriana, if you don't want to..." He trailed off.

He'd asked a simple question. One that should have been safe for small talk, Adriana knew.

But there was no way she could explain how she'd ended up with the job without going this far back.

She shrugged like it didn't matter. Like she didn't hesitate to open up like this.

"Really," Levi said again, his voice firm.

Maybe he didn't want to know. Or didn't want to know her?

"Anyway, I heard about the concept of using dogs for searches when a student disappeared from our campus and then was found because of a dog. That stuck with me and later on, after Robert died, I decided that was what I wanted to do with my life." She kept her voice light and gave him the CliffsNotes version.

Then why did she feel a sting, like she'd come close to having someone to trust with her whole story?

She looked ahead, watched Blue's shoulders tense.

Come on, girl. Find it. Do you have the scent?

Still, the dog didn't alert. But she did pick up her pace. Adriana picked hers up to match, careful not to look at the man beside her who was, and would always be, strictly a coworker.

Because right now, her tense relationship with him, her feelings about the past, her desire to have someone want to know her: none of that mattered. Somewhere in these dark spruce woods, Levi believed there was a new body. That would not only provide another starting point for his investigation, it would also bring with it the heartache of knowing someone else had lost a family member.

The least she could do was bring closure.

Adriana watched the dog closely and kept walking.

SEVEN

Levi had done something wrong or said something wrong, that much he'd figured out. But what, he wasn't sure. For now, it was all he could do to keep up with Adriana and her dog. They were walking through an area where the trail had narrowed. He could still walk beside Adriana, but only barely. He was fascinated by her use of the dog and wanted to see how the whole thing worked.

So far all he'd seen was a dog on a hike through the woods, off-leash. Blue had sped up a little, but did that mean anything? Levi wasn't sure. He wasn't sure about any of this, really. Not that he was a critic. He believed she could help, didn't he? He was counting on her.

But it was still a bit hard to imagine, that a dog could…

The dog barked.

"Is that the alert?" He turned to Adriana. Her eyes were straight ahead, on the dog. She was focused and alert, with no hint of a smile. The opposite of relaxed.

"We'll talk later, okay? Or not, Levi. Whichever you prefer, but right now I am working."

Ouch. Yeah, he had definitely said something wrong. And later he'd figure out what, but right now her dog had taken off and she was running, too. Levi ran after them, hand on the sidearm he wore on his hip. He was pressing it against himself to keep it from bouncing around.

The dog took a bend in the trail to the left and Adriana and Levi were close behind. Then Blue took off into the woods. Adriana was pushing past branches and Levi kept his hands out to deflect them, since she was in such a hurry she wasn't slowing them down as she pushed through.

And he didn't blame her. Since the dog

usually kept her in sight, this was extremely odd behavior.

They all kept running. For two more minutes? Five? Levi didn't know, only knew that he was glad he made outdoor recreation and being in shape such a high priority because their pace was intense.

The dog skidded to a stop, then started pacing. Whining.

Adriana bent down next to the husky, to catch her breath, it looked like.

Levi stayed back and waited, looking around to make sure they were alone. Though the woods were thick with trees and he didn't see anyone else around them, he didn't feel protected. He felt exposed.

Worse, he was worried Adriana could be in danger.

The further into the woods they hiked, the more their options for escape were limited. Alaska's woods weren't as thick with brush as some he'd hiked in during his time in the Lower 48, but they still had their fair share of weeds and brush. Here, tall devil's club and cow parsnip still bloomed, their branches reaching almost as tall as he was. In an emergency, they would block many of the other possible trails.

Levi glanced at Adriana. If it came down to it, she'd have the presence of mind to run. But that didn't matter if they got so deep into the woods that there was nowhere to run.

He looked around. Again, nothing out of the ordinary.

Still, a sense of foreboding pressed on his chest. The darker the woods got, the worse the feeling grew.

"What did she find?"

The dog whined again, then lay down.

Adriana looked at her, then back up at him. "She found exactly what we came to look for."

Levi raised his eyebrows. An hour of hiking and they'd found the body the killer must have been burying when the hiker stumbled across them? It seemed too good to be true. His eyes narrowed.

"Unless..."

Surely there was no way to confuse a search dog, right?

Also, shouldn't the ground be messed up? Obviously dug up and then recovered? If the hiker who had disappeared had walked up on a body being buried, it should be freshly buried enough that the ground wouldn't have settled.

If this was a body, it had been here much longer than a week.

Was there more than one body in these woods?

What had he walked Adriana into?

"Get down," he ordered her, not stopping to think about anything aside from what was happening right now and the uncomfortable feeling he had that something was wrong.

Adriana frowned and kept standing. "Levi…"

"Down," he said again, this time more firmly, just short of raising his voice, but in a way that was clear he meant what he said.

She called Blue to her, rubbed her ears

and crouched beside her. Levi moved toward them, ready to shield her with his body if necessary, but...

Nothing happened.

No gunshots. No crashes through the trees.

Nothing.

"What's wrong?" Her voice didn't waver, so she must have trusted him; that much was clear in the steady tone of her voice.

And Levi didn't know how to answer her.

Was it just him? He'd never reacted like this before.

"I..." Nope, he still had no good explanation.

"Am I okay to stand back up? Because kneeling beside a buried body really makes me uncomfortable."

"Yes, sorry, go ahead."

"What's wrong, Levi?" Adriana stood back up carefully, looking around like she was keeping her eyes open for anything strange.

He had overreacted.

Yesterday's conversation with Judah was haunting him now. His brother had told him he had no business letting a civilian help him. Maybe it wasn't just because Judah was concerned that doing so would be dangerous for Adriana. Maybe he'd also been able to tell that Levi wouldn't be able to avoid making this personal.

He'd just started to get to know her yesterday and today. At the very least, as a friend, a coworker, she intrigued him. And also kept him on his toes. He didn't have anyone to do that for him very often.

It made sense he'd been extra jumpy.

"Levi?"

"Sorry." He shook his head. "I thought I saw something, but I didn't."

She studied him for a moment. For signs that he was falling apart? After a short time, she nodded, then continued. "So," she began, "what now?"

"This is supposed to be a body? Buried right here?"

Adriana nodded.

"But it's not fresh."

"Right. So you have two choices." She was keeping her voice quiet, but it still echoed in the chilly autumn woods, without summer's full leaves on all the trees to insulate their words. The echo gave him chills and made him wish he could whisk her away somewhere safer.

He wasn't sure what she meant. "Okay…"

"Either our guess was wrong, and the killer didn't get caught burying a body and then murder the hiker, or he or she did get caught, but not burying this body. Or—I guess this is three choices—the hiker got too close to this spot and it made the killer nervous, though why he would be here essentially guarding a burial site I don't know. So that option is my least favorite."

She had a head for this, he realized. How much of that was because there were commonalities between working a search-and-rescue mission and solving a crime? Levi wasn't sure, but she impressed him.

He nodded, testing out the theories for size in his mind. "All right, I can see those, though I agree you're right—the last is the least likely."

"For now, though." Now it was her turn to seem uncomfortable. She looked around nervously. "Could we handle this and get back somewhere inside and well lit? This whole place is frankly kind of creepy, knowing what we are standing on or near."

Levi raised his eyebrows. *Huh...* He wouldn't have thought she would be bothered.

She shrugged. "I can help Blue find them, but I don't really love the whole thought of what we are doing if I think too hard about it."

"That's fair." Levi pulled his phone from his pocket. "Let me call this in and get a team out here to excavate the body."

"Should we mark it or something?" Adriana asked. He was already pulling out his GPS device, which he'd used many times in the backcountry just exploring, but it would also come in handy now.

"I'll mark the coordinates. A team will come out as soon as they can. I'm messaging them and the police department now."

"What kind of team?" she asked.

He did his best to answer while getting the coordinates marked. "It's really just someone I know..." He trailed off and finished what he was doing, then looked back up at her. "In Anchorage. She's a forensic pathologist and she's qualified for this kind of work."

"Makes sense."

Levi put the device back in his pocket. "Ready?"

"Ready for what?"

"In case our suspicion earlier was correct, that the hiker was killed because she stumbled on a recent burial, we should keep searching. We should hike around some more. If there is a body here—"

"What do you mean, if?" She sounded annoyed, he noted. "If Blue alerts, there is a body."

"I just don't want to jump to conclusions."

"She's a cadaver dog, Levi. She knows what she found. Give her the benefit of the doubt here."

Levi considered it for a minute and then nodded. "Okay, even though there's a body here, it's not the one we are looking for. If the hiker was killed because of a recent murder or burial, the ground would be more disturbed. The scene would be fresh."

Adriana nodded.

"Is there a way to, like, clear the dog?" Levi asked, looking down at the husky, who had set down her head on her paws, brown eyes looking mournful.

Did the dogs know what they found? He found himself wondering. That would be tough on them, he imagined.

"Clear the dog?" Adriana's eyebrows were raised and if he wasn't mistaken, she was trying to suppress a smile.

And failing. Quite spectacularly.

Levi shrugged. "Reset her? I don't know,

tell her to try again? Is there a way to say 'Yes, good dog, that was a body, can you find another?' Or is it like a once-per-day kind of thing?"

He had expected her to look at him while he talked, but she was gazing at the dog and he found he didn't mind. Actually it fascinated him, her partnership with the dog and the way she had a working dog whose needs she was so in tune with.

"I think another today would be fine. We can't do too many at once because it can depress them, but she could probably look for one more and see what we turn up. Hopefully that will be enough for today."

She looked so hopeful that Levi didn't want to point out all the things that could go wrong. Like, for example, this body might not belong to a serial killer's victim at all. It could be much older. He knew from the Google search he'd done on search-and-rescue dogs last night that they could recover even much older remains. This may not be one of the sites they were looking for at all.

But it might be. And he hoped it was. Especially because Adriana looked like she needed a win.

So did her dog.

"Come on, Blue," she said gently, moving the K9 away from her place on the ground. Once she was twenty feet away or so, back on the trail—Levi had followed her—she stopped and petted the dog, then reached into her pocket and showed Blue a toy.

Blue wagged her tail and her eyes looked slightly less sad.

"Yeah, you get a new toy, don't you, good girl? You did such a good job today."

"Does the baby voice help?" He did nothing to keep the amusement from his voice.

Adriana wrapped her arms around the huge white animal. "Listen, if it makes my baby happy and my baby keeps doing this job for you, I don't think you should mind."

She had a point. But it was still cute. Levi laughed.

"All right, ready?" she asked the dog, then bent down toward it. Had she said something? Given some kind of command?

Levi wasn't sure, but the dog moved down the trail farther, ignoring the site they had left behind.

"Can we walk toward the lake on purpose? Will that throw off her search?" He was keeping in mind the fact that he really didn't know what kinds of remains were in these woods to discover. If the serial killer had dumped the hiker in the lake rather than bury her, it would make sense for the lake to have been extraordinarily convenient.

"If that's the area where we want her to search that's fine. We can move that way."

Adriana moved to her dog and called her that direction, then headed toward the lake, on the right-hand side of the woods.

The dog's pace picked up slightly, but

not enough that Levi was sure if she'd smelled something.

Of all the things he'd seen during the years he'd been doing police work, this was unquestionably one of the most interesting. While he had worked on cases with the SAR team before, and even seen Adriana and her dogs at work, he'd never paid *this* much attention. It was almost unbelievable, except he was seeing it, and did believe it.

He followed behind silently and they hiked for about another ten minutes. The dog's pace seemed to vary. She would slow, then speed up.

Finally her speed increased dramatically, just like the last time, and she let out a bark as she hurried for some unseen spot ahead. She turned back around, ran to Adriana, then ran back up ahead.

"Legit, that's just like Lassie," he said, remembering old reruns he'd watched as a kid at his grandma's house.

"Good girl, Blue." Adriana ignored Levi for now and followed her dog.

Levi followed both of them.

Please, let this be near the lake. Really, really near, Levi prayed.

They twisted through trees, fallen leaves crunching underneath their feet, toward what he had to hope was a body because they needed to solve this case and it would be another lead. According to what Adriana said earlier, it had to be. She believed if her dog alerted, it was surely a body.

Still, he hated to know it was another body because even as he thought it, his chest stabbed with hurt for some family out there that was already missing a relative. And whose hopes for a living person were about to be crushed.

Adriana couldn't possibly be more proud of her dog.

As a general rule, Blue didn't find more than one body a day. There just wasn't a need for it as they were usually searching for one missing person, and so she just didn't have the opportunity. She'd heard about the working dogs of 9/11 and the way some of them burned out and were depressed after the carnage they saw; she'd always been thankful she didn't have to worry about that with hers.

But two in one day seemed like it would be okay and so she'd taken a calculated risk in letting the dog continue on.

Blue dropped to her stomach and whined at the ground—it was a patch of earth that sat on a slight rise, overlooking the lake.

It was a spot that would be perfect for someone to bury one body, then dump another into the lake if discovered.

She was so, so proud.

"Good girl, Blue." She kneeled next to her K9, rubbed her ears. And looked back at Levi.

He looked as happy as she felt. Their theory had just gotten more plausible.

"Is it fresh, though?" Adriana looked at it.

Levi walked over, gently nudged some of the leaves with his foot.

The spot did seem to have more leaves over it than the rest of the area. In fact, some of the trees had less foliage underneath them than she would have expected.

He scraped the leaves away from the spot next to Blue.

The ground underneath was freshly patted down. Like someone had dug it up with a shovel and then smoothed it back out.

Then covered it with leaves.

The wind whistled through the trees, rustling a few fallen leaves up from the ground, and Adriana shivered.

"Good girl," she told the dog again.

It was easier in some ways for animals to find a missing person. When a person was rescued by a search dog they tended to be thankful, excited, and that passed onto the dog. When a cadaver was found, the energy was completely different. And the dogs noticed.

Levi was marking the coordinates on his GPS tracker again.

"When is your friend coming? Did you say where she's from?" Adriana couldn't remember.

"Anchorage. But she headed down earlier today when I told her I thought we might find something. So she's staying in Raven Pass and should be here soon."

Like talking about it had made it happen faster, Levi's phone rang then. He gave someone directions to where they were, then hung up.

"That was her?"

"Yes."

Adriana nodded. Should it bother her that him having a female friend he talked about made her feel almost...? Not, like, jealous, but...

"So tell me about your friend," she finally said, hoping her voice stayed normal.

"Wren is actually my cousin," he said as he lowered himself down to sit against the base of a tree.

Oh. Cousin.

There was no reason for Adriana to feel relieved, but...

Okay, sure, yes. She felt relieved.

He was a handsome, outdoorsy man who had a desire to bring justice to the world. And she wasn't completely immune to that. Especially now that she had spent enough time with him to realize that some of her assumptions about him had been off.

Levi was on the phone now with the police department, judging by his end of the conversation that she was overhearing. When he hung up, he turned back to her.

"She always wanted to be a forensic anthropologist, and when she got her degree, she found a job up here." He shrugged.

"Are you from Alaska? I can't remember," she admitted.

Levi nodded. "From Anchorage, originally. Judah moved here first, then me."

"It didn't bother you to follow your brother?"

He raised his eyebrows and she wished for a minute she hadn't asked. "Sorry—"

"No, it's okay." He looked away from her, then back again. "I know what you're asking. And in some ways, yes. But it's also worth it to be around family. However much of a hard time they can give me."

Not something she understood at all, but she didn't know him nearly well enough to open up that can of worms. Talking about her loss of Robert was one thing. Her family was definitely like a twentieth-date kind of topic.

Or twentieth year of marriage. She would be okay just not talking about them for that long.

Sudden noises in the forest drew both of their attention. A crackling branch? A rustling leaf? The noises were just small enough Adriana couldn't identify what they were, and they might not be out of place, but in a situation like this it was still enough to make her jumpy. Adriana looked up, back toward the direction from where they'd come.

Levi had stood up, had his hand on his side. Over a weapon? She couldn't see but guessed so. Even though it was likely it was Wren, she appreciated that he was being careful and not taking any chances.

Even if it did lead to some odd situations, like earlier when he'd told her to get down and nothing had happened.

A small woman with blond hair tangled around her shoulders looked up and smiled. "You must be Adriana. Levi, good to see you."

"Thanks for coming." He walked over in her direction.

"Is this the scene?" She gestured in front of them to the forest floor.

Levi answered. "Yes. Adriana's dog found it."

"How does that work?" Wren seemed genuinely curious.

"She alerts to the spot by barking and lying down." Adriana motioned to Blue, who was still lying down. "Come here, girl," Adriana called her to her and Blue looked back at the spot but then ran to her.

Carefully, Wren started to work. She cleared the area first, after suggesting that Levi check it for evidence that might have been left, which he already had. As she meticulously removed the leaves and then started to measure the approximate area,

Adriana watched her. Seeing her work was fascinating, but Blue looked like she needed a break. Her ears drooped a little more than usual and her eyes looked sad.

"I need to take Blue somewhere else." They didn't usually stick around for this long and she wasn't comfortable with the dog's mood. If they stayed too long, she could get depressed.

"I can come with you in a few minutes. I'm still waiting for another officer." He glanced at Wren. "I don't want either of you alone right now."

Which made sense to Adriana. While neither of them was at a coffee shop, they did fit the profile of the victims. It would be wise to be extra careful, rather than getting into trouble.

But her dog couldn't wait much longer.

Thankfully, another officer walked up after only a few minutes.

"This is Officer Quinn Koser."

"Nice to meet you," Adriana and Wren said at the same time.

"I've really got to go." Adriana glanced at Levi. "Sorry."

She put a leash on Blue and headed into the thick woods, back onto the trail. She could hear Levi behind her, could feel him watching her, but never glanced back.

"You okay?" he finally asked.

Was she? Blue's mood seemed to have affected her. Or maybe it was the other way around. All she knew was that this wasn't the type of work she wanted to do all the time.

"I don't know," she finally answered honestly, then shrugged as she inhaled a deep breath. The air was crisp and cool.

"You did good today." He said it and then walked along quietly, maybe sensing she needed the space.

No matter how many deep breaths she took, though, her head didn't clear. It felt fuzzy. Like there was too much pressure in it.

She kept walking. Kept breathing. She felt him behind her.

One thing Adriana appreciated was the

fact that he seemed to understand that she couldn't put her feelings into words if she tried. She liked that he didn't try to keep talking until it made sense, or until she could say what was wrong.

Maybe that was the reason she liked hanging out with her dogs so much. Most people pressed for answers. Levi didn't seem to be like that.

Interesting.

She kept walking in silence until the clearing at the end of the trail, where the parking lot was, came in sight. Then, finally, she exhaled, feeling her spirit lighten as the sunshine found its way through the trees more.

"I think it's just that... I don't know. It affected me more than I thought."

"Finding murder victims?"

When he did talk, he didn't mince words. He got right to the point, to the center of the issue at hand.

And yet she somehow didn't wish that she was alone with her dogs. It was right that he was here.

"Yes." She nodded. "Someone did this."

"Someone did."

And as she inhaled, she felt herself become even more determined to solve it.

She looked up at Levi, admiration building in her. She'd thought he was laid-back, didn't take things seriously enough.

How much of that was self-protection? Was he just trying to keep his work from weighing him down?

After spending today doing this work with him, it seemed like that.

It was possible, very possible, that she'd misjudged him.

And that thought was dangerous to her in an entirely different way than a killer who might be after them both.

EIGHT

Levi had wanted, with almost everything in him, to stay at the crime scene. This was his case, and he was finally getting somewhere. He felt like they were closer now than they'd ever been to ending this.

The idea that the killer had been targeting victims years before, when Levi himself was still a kid, was still mind-blowing, even though the idea'd had a couple of days to sink in. The initial cases he'd found in the cold case file had been women whose bodies had been found, whom investigators had linked to a common serial killer. And now there seemed to be a link to the four bodies he'd been investigating for the last few years. Were there more buried somewhere? Had the killer committed any other murders in all those intermittent years? Or had there truly been a pause?

And if the latter was true, then why?

Much as he'd wanted to stay, he knew he could count on Officer Koser to handle it and he needed to get Adriana home. She wasn't a responsibility he could delegate, not with the possible threat against her. He was still fairly certain the attacks had been against him, but she was working with him now. He couldn't afford to take chances, not where her safety was concerned.

"Thanks for driving me home." She'd finally spoken as he pulled into her driveway.

Levi nodded, half of his mind in the present, half back there in the woods wondering what Wren was finding right now and how it would change how they worked this case.

If they got a break now, it wasn't because he'd earned it, but he'd take it anyway. He'd thought that morning that he would come up with a solid plan for how to approach this, but Adriana had offered different ideas—good ones—and then he'd had some of his own realizations, and at the end of the day, nothing had gone as he could have predicted.

Was that good or bad?

That was something he'd have to think about more. Right now, his mind couldn't handle a single other thought than all the ones he'd stuffed into it throughout the day.

"Thanks for all your help today," he finally said.

"Do you want to come in? I could make coffee," she offered.

It was the first solid olive branch she'd proffered since he'd done or said something to offend her in the woods hours earlier, before Blue had alerted to the first body. What had they been talking about? He'd asked how she'd chosen her career and become a search-and-rescue dog handler.

Nope, he still couldn't figure out what

he'd said wrong there. Unless it had something to do with the loss of her fiancé? But it had seemed like more than that. Either way she'd pulled back, for sure. Now she was asking him to come inside for coffee.

Did he say yes?

He glanced in her direction, trying to figure out if this was an obligatory kind of invite, or if maybe she was scared to be alone. But, no, he saw no fear in her dark brown eyes, just a tiny spark of friendship, or what could be friendship if he didn't mess it up.

"I can't stay long, but I'd love to for a little while if that's okay." The words were out of his mouth before he'd finished deciding that's what he was going to do.

Adriana nodded. "Okay."

She led the way to the front door and let them both in with a key. "So coffee?" she offered.

This time, he shook his head. "No, but water would be great. You don't have to get it, I saw where the cups were last night."

She looked like she wanted to argue for half a second, and that's when he remembered she'd said she was from down south somewhere. Maybe down there people served guests, but up here in Alaska, at least among Levi and his friends, it was a sign of real friendship to know where things were and serve yourself.

He watched her let Blue off her leash. The dog happily bounded into the house and was quickly joined by Adriana's other dog. Adriana pulled another toy out of her vest pocket, one he hadn't seen earlier.

"You're such a good girl. The best girl." She handed the dog the toy and Blue ran off with it, looking half the age she had earlier.

"And you're the best boy," Adriana told the second dog—Babe, he thought his name was—and that one ran off also.

"Blue seemed different earlier," he commented aloud.

"Bodies depress her."

And her owner, too, unless he'd missed his guess about Adriana's reaction earlier.

She'd seemed shaken, especially after the discovery of the second body.

"Is she still okay to search tomorrow or does she need a day off?"

She looked at him with surprise. He tried to read what was behind her eyes, but couldn't.

"I don't want to make this take any longer than it has to."

Levi opened his mouth to reply, but his phone rang before he could. He made an apologetic face. "I'm sorry, just one second, okay?" He didn't like to answer calls when he was in midconversation, but they were in the middle of a case. It was necessary.

"Wicks, it's Koser."

"Thanks for calling, what did you find?"

"It was a woman. Midtwenties, probably. Blond hair. Her prints are in the system—Raina Marston."

If he was mentioning hair, it must not have been an old body. The chances had just gone up that this had been the site and victim they assumed might be there—

the one that presumably Lara Jones had stumbled on, maybe even seen the killer burying, that had led to the hiker's death.

"Why do we have her prints, do we know?"

"Looks like she was printed for a substitute job with a school district."

"Okay." Levi took a deep breath. "What else?" He waited, wondering what else they had learned.

"Zip tie around her hands. Orange. Same brand as the others."

Levi knew most of the officers at Raven Pass PD were familiar with the case, even though he'd been the one primarily working on it. Quinn knew the orange zip ties were part of their serial killer's MO.

"Can we establish any kind of time of death yet?" Levi asked, thinking that the ME probably hadn't gotten there yet. Only the medical examiner could establish an approximation with any kind of certainty. That was one of their specialties.

"The ME just got here. He won't say

for sure yet, but these aren't old bones, Wicks."

So very, very likely their theory about the hiker interrupting a burial was correct.

Which would mean adding a fifth body to the serial killer's recent tally.

And there was still the body that Blue had found first today to consider. Was it coincidence the two were buried in the woods? Or had the killer buried them together in the same general location?

And if he had…

Were there more? Were all the burial sites by twos and they only had half the victims accounted for? Even though Raina's body and the other hadn't been in close proximity, they'd been located within half a mile of each other.

It was a terrifying thought.

Levi felt Adriana watching him and wondered how many of his thoughts she could read on his face. He held up one finger in a one-sec kind of sign and walked toward her front door, back into the entryway, where he'd have a little privacy.

"Has anyone been able to work on the scene we found first?" He'd called that in, too, along with the coordinates he'd marked, but it had been necessary to start with the most recent burial. Vital evidence was more likely to be found in the most recently killed body.

"Not yet, but I'll keep you posted. I just wanted you to know this part. The ME is taking her to Anchorage."

"Thanks, man, I appreciate it."

"All right. Bye."

Levi hung up the phone and stood for a minute, thinking.

The serial killer had killed again. A blonde woman, midtwenties. They'd know more soon, hopefully.

But the thought of the killer burying bodies in twos still lingered. Was there a possibility that more bodies were buried in twos? Maybe one older corpse and one more recent? That was just a guess as he didn't know anything about one of the two they'd found that day, but it was possible. Worth investigating further.

Tomorrow, they'd give the dog a break and spend the day finding out all they could about Raina Marston. But the next day, they'd go check the four sites where he'd found bodies before, and see if they'd been the only ones buried there.

Adriana had been running through the day in her mind, over and over, while she drank her coffee, but she still couldn't truly make sense of it or reconcile her mind to it.

She hated the fact that people killed other people. Yet she knew it was true. She'd seen enough violence during her time in Oklahoma to know that and had lost one of her favorite cousins to senseless violence.

That was when she decided she'd follow Robert to Alaska and never look back. She'd needed to distance herself from everything back home and Alaska had seemed like a pretty good place to do it.

Then, when she'd lost Robert, becoming a search-dog handler and reinventing herself had seemed like a good idea, too.

This—helping out Levi—was a little too close to reminding her of everything she'd tried to escape.

Pasts, she knew better than most in her line of work, did not stay buried well.

"Sorry about that," Levi said when he walked back in. "That was Officer Koser, the guy we left there."

"What did he say?" Because news, she could handle more of. Anything that told her this would be over soon.

"We know the woman's identity, and if it is okay with you I think we should spend tomorrow talking to her family and trying to establish what we know about her."

"Is that a step backward in the case, though?"

"No, I don't think so."

"Okay, if you're sure." Adriana couldn't deny that a day with less adventure sounded good to her. It would still be emotionally exhausting, she knew from experience with the SAR team, to talk to the bereaved family. But it was still easier than going out and looking for more bodies.

She could use something a little easier after today.

From her place in the passenger seat of Levi's car the next morning, Adriana's eyes widened and she gripped her coffee tighter. The earth on the other side of Levi's car dropped off into a ravine, the road itself literally crumbling at the edges into…

Well, air.

No guardrails. That would provide an illusion of some kind of safety. Adriana swallowed hard and tried to ignore the pressure in her chest. She was not having a panic attack today, definitely not in front of Levi, where he sat at the wheel calmly driving the road to Raina Marston's parents' house like it was a normal subdivision road.

She guessed the sign at the entrance that said Wilderness Heights should have been her first clue. It was definitely wilderness. And they were very, very high up.

This was not what she'd been expecting.

Adriana set down her coffee in a cup holder, not taking her eyes from the road. Now she gripped the top of her to-go coffee cup with her left hand and the handhold grip of the car door with the other.

"It's really fine." Levi glanced in her direction.

"Do not look at me, look at the road!"

So, yes, she was scared of heights. She may have left that tidbit out of her aboutme section because really, who hired a search-and-rescue team member who was scared of heights? It didn't affect how good a job she did as she was always able to push through the fear when a search required it, but she still hated it, like her own personal thorn in her flesh.

"Hey." His voice was quieter now. She felt his hand settle on top of hers. Warm. Strong. "It is going to be okay."

Simple words like that shouldn't have the power to release the tension from her shoulders, to ease the grip she had on the handhold. No, instead she should be embarrassed that much as she may have tried to keep her acrophobia a secret, Levi had just uncovered it.

But she wasn't. She felt…similar to yesterday. Known.

Adriana swallowed hard as something awfully similar to butterflies danced in her stomach and not from the height. It had been so many years since she'd felt more than a passing bond with someone. This felt…like more than passing.

The second she'd decided she liked his hand there, that maybe she was ready to take the risk to open her heart just a tiny bit, he yanked it away. Like somehow he hadn't been conscious of what he had done until that very second and now he was, and regretted it.

"I'm sorry." He shook his head. "I shouldn't… Yeah." He cleared his throat. "This is their house, on the right."

Better than on the left. Because even though it meant they had a steep driveway to drive up, they weren't driving essentially off a cliff, so she was thankful for that.

"So what's the plan when we go in there?" Mainly she asked to try to keep her mind focused on what they were doing, instead of imagining the possibility of something developing with Levi.

She still wasn't sure why she'd come today. She appreciated his understanding about Blue needing a day off. They'd pick up looking for burial grounds tomorrow. But why did she need to be here? She wasn't a regular partner, not in any sense of the word.

Unless it informed the search somehow? Adriana guessed she could see how that would be a possibility. And it was always better to have a second set of ears hearing people talk, in case someone missed something.

"I just want to talk to them and see what insights they can offer. Sometimes the tiniest details end up being useful to a case. Besides, don't you think they deserve to know that someone is looking for their daughter's killer?"

Yes, of course she thought so. She wanted them to have closure.

Did that mean she was ready to go look people facing loss in the eyes?

No, not at all.

Yet he was reaching for the door handle, clearly expecting her to follow. "Ready?"

No. Yes? She would try to be. Rather than say any of it, Adriana nodded. She was as ready as she was going to be.

Levi opened his door and stepped out and Adriana did the same. The air was a little warmer today, almost like a Lower-48 fall day, and the sun was shining, clear and bright in a vibrant blue sky.

She loved Alaska. Had since the first day she'd stepped out of the Ted Stevens Anchorage International Airport. She might be from Oklahoma, but she was pretty sure somehow that she was Alaskan at heart.

They walked to the front door, rang the bell.

A woman, probably in her midsixties, answered. She looked like someone who had been crying, but who had tried to pull herself together. Adriana knew Levi had called yesterday to set up this appointment, so at least they weren't showing up unannounced, but she still felt uncomfortable stepping into someone else's grief when she always wanted to be left alone with hers.

"Mrs. Marston?" Levi held out a hand, and Adriana noticed not for the first time how much of an impression he made in his tan Raven Pass Police Department uniform. She'd seen him in it before, obviously. But he didn't wear it every time he worked. She guessed an occasion like this called for it, to lend some legitimacy to their coming by, and maybe to reassure people, too. That the police were working on things. That their daughter's killer wasn't going to be left to roam free.

Mrs. Marston's face relaxed into something resembling trust as she took in Levi's appearance and nodded her head. Her shoulders relaxed, like his being here was a reassurance in and of itself.

"You must be Officer Wicks. Thank you for coming by. We are glad to get to talk to you. My husband is upstairs and should be down in a few minutes."

The words, about being glad they could talk to him, struck Adriana as odd. They wanted to talk about things? Maybe some people did better when they talked about what was hurting them.

"This is Adriana Steele. She's part of the Raven Pass SAR team—search and rescue—and her dog was responsible for finding your daughter's body."

She felt herself bristle, though she held out her hand and attempted a smile. Surely learning that Blue had discovered the body wouldn't bring the woman joy the way search dogs did when they found people who were alive and had just been waiting for rescue. Maybe it was silly to feel so overprotective of her dogs, but she didn't want anyone thinking badly of them.

"We are so thankful for you, dear. And your dog. To have had no closure…" She stopped talking, then took a shuddery breath and sniffed. "We are glad you do what you do. What a difficult job."

The woman's words sounded genuine, despite the fact that they were foreign to Adriana.

"Thank you."

It was all she could say, the only words she could force from her lips. She tried another small smile and prayed that Levi would take the lead with the conversation here because being in a room this heavy, with grief that didn't feel suffocating or dark, was confusing her.

"Sorry about that. I'm Dave Marston." A man about the same age and height as his wife came down the stairs and walked toward them, holding out his hand for both of them to shake.

"Thanks for meeting with us," Levi said.

The man's face was a little harder to read, but he nodded. "Thank you for coming by."

Strange, how everyone handled grief in different ways.

"Please, come in and sit. Would anyone like coffee?"

Adriana couldn't drink anything. Not right now, when she could barely even focus on taking breaths, in and out.

"I'm okay, thank you," she said, wondering if that counted as a lie.

Levi glanced at her, a strange sideways glance.

"I would love a cup," he answered, still looking as relaxed as if they were...well, anywhere but here.

Mrs. Marston poured it for him and then they sat in the living room. Adriana sat down first, at one end of a couch, and Levi sat beside her. Not on the other end, as she would have expected, but right beside her. Close enough to reach out to for support, except she wouldn't do that, and shouldn't even think that way.

She wasn't the only one who had a past, that much was clear to her. Something had happened to Levi to make him hesitant to trust.

And despite the fact that it wasn't her

business, not as someone who only occasionally saw him in a work capacity, Adriana wanted to know.

She felt awareness of him spread through the blush on her cheeks, and she swallowed hard.

Levi cleared his throat and began. "Mr. and Mrs. Marston, I wanted to say first that we are sorry for your loss."

They both nodded. "Thank you."

Levi took another sip of coffee. "Your daughter seems like she was a wonderful person. I looked at her social-media profiles a bit last night. You were really blessed with her, I think."

What on earth? Did he think this was a good tactic, reminding them of all they had lost? Adriana felt herself pull away again. Only internally. Externally they were still sitting almost close enough to touch.

But how could he talk about Raina like this, like she was still there, sitting in the living room with them, instead of in a morgue somewhere, probably mid-autopsy? Gone forever.

Adriana was not surprised at all to watch Mrs. Marston's eyes pool with un-shed tears. But she was surprised at what she said. "Thank you. Thank you for seeing her as more than a victim, and for your words. So many people..." The tears fell now. "So many people haven't said anything."

"They don't know what to say," Mr. Marston said to his wife, in a tone that made it sound like this was something he'd said before.

"I know, but..." She sniffed again. "Thank you."

Levi nodded. His face remained unreadable, but Adriana wondered how he did this. And then found herself wondering how *often* he did this. She'd never once considered the feelings of the law-enforcement officers who had to deliver bad news over and over, who saw people on their worst days.

But they had to be made of something

special, or gifted by God in some way. She usually slipped away before other people got involved, in the guise of Blue needing a break.

Truly, it was Adriana who wouldn't stand that close to death for too long without feeling it threaten to overtake her hope.

Her dog held it together better than she did.

She didn't hear most of what was said for the next ten minutes. She tried—she really did. But she was overwhelmed. Why had this all started to affect her so much? For years, she'd been fine.

She wanted to pull out her phone and text someone. Ellie, maybe. While Adriana had held herself at arm's length from the other members of her SAR team, she and Ellie had connected a bit more. Maybe because Adriana was under the impression that Ellie was hiding things from her past also. Not bad things, but personal ones.

Shadows. Darkness.

Oh, how familiar Adriana was with those.

Okay, no, she hadn't "dealt" with her feelings like some friends had suggested. She hadn't talked to a counselor, or anyone who didn't have four legs and a tail. She was pretty sure the late-night conversations she had with her dogs weren't what her friends had in mind.

"Can you tell me more about your daughter? Any friends she had that might help us track down her killer, places she hung out?" Adriana heard Levi ask the questions as she tried to focus back in.

Something flickered on the face of both Marstons.

Something, some internal nudge, told her that these people held the answers she was looking for. They were facing death without flinching, facing loss and still looking ahead to their future.

As she held her breath and waited for their answer, she wondered for the first time if one day she could get there, too. To a point where she could only look forward and not be constantly pulled back to her past.

To be here, to be listening to them, was like being emotionally unprotected. Vulnerable.

And sitting next to Levi made that feel even truer. The man had seen her at her worst more than anyone else had.

But nevertheless, Adriana was ready. She leaned forward to listen.

Ready, maybe for the first time, to find out how to move forward with her own life—and the case itself.

NINE

"We've told the police everything already, when Officer Koser and Officer Smith came by right after they positively identified her body," Mr. Marston began, after clearing his throat, "but something about the way you asked reminded me they mostly asked about where she was the day she disappeared."

Levi had read the reports already. Raina had been at work, at a nearby elementary school, the day she disappeared. People had seen her until just after four, when she'd left. She hadn't shown up to a Pilates class at seven. There were hardly any traffic cameras in the area, since Raven Pass had one stoplight and even it was fairly unnecessary, so looking at that hadn't yielded results. They'd asked on social media, had run the search from every angle they could think of.

But the three-hour window remained.

"She was at school, right?" he asked to prompt Raina's father, though he started to question his coming here. These people were grieving.

His time might be better spent elsewhere. Even while he waited for the man to speak, he began to plan his exit strategy.

"But it's where she didn't go that is interesting to me."

Levi looked up. Waited.

"We talked to her that morning, just a few texts. She was talking about how riled up her students were, and that she hadn't had coffee. She'd been running late. Now, she may have had it at school—teacher's lounges have coffee makers, you know, but..." He glanced at his wife. "Maybe she stopped at her favorite coffee shop after school."

"Which was?"

"Raven's Rest. The one on Second

Street, near the woods." He shook his head. "It seems like an awfully easy place to go missing."

Levi perked up at that comment. He had said nothing about the pattern of women to disappear from coffee shops in this area.

So there was no reason for the Marstons to link the coffee shop for that reason. But the fact that Raina's dad had remembered she'd not had coffee that day was important.

"I do appreciate knowing that." He kept his voice even so he wouldn't give them false hope if this lead didn't go anywhere.

But they had just given him something to work with.

They talked for a little longer. Levi did his best to update them on the progress of the case and to listen. Adriana joined in very little and unless he missed his guess, he thought she might be a little pale.

She'd lost her fiancé. She'd told him that the other day, but her anxiety was bigger than even her panic attacks, wasn't it? It had been years ago, surely...

No, there was no time limit on things like that. He knew that better than most. He might never be like a guy who hadn't gone through what he'd gone through, no matter how many years passed between his wife's infidelity, and then desertion, and now.

No, what people went through changed them. Forever.

"Thank you again for your time." He told the Marstons when they'd wrapped up their conversation and been through the careful dance of "thanks for coming," "thanks for having us," and all that society had declared had to happen before a conversation could end. They'd all moved to the entryway and then back to the front deck.

"Thank you. We really liked talking about her." Mrs. Marston's smile was genuine, even with the tearstains on her cheeks. "I appreciate what you are doing to find whoever...did this." She glanced over at Adriana, then looked straight at Levi. "Be careful. And make sure that she is careful." The older woman nodded, like she'd given him some kind of official order.

"Whoever did this is still out there. I can't see them appreciating being caught."

"Adriana, could I talk to you alone, just for a minute?" Mrs. Marston asked as they crossed the deck.

Levi's eyebrows rose and Mrs. Marston shook her head. "Just here, on the deck. I know you probably don't want to let her out of your sight at all. I know my daughter isn't the first young woman to disappear here in the last decade."

Adriana nodded, so Levi nodded, too. Adriana did fit the profile, though in her late twenties she was slightly older than many of them. Mostly he didn't want her out of his sight because of the direct threats against both of them.

"I'll go start the car," he said, watching out of the corner of his eye as he walked away.

What would it be like, he wondered, to have been involved with a woman who would still grieve years after he died?

Not that he would ever want to cause someone that much grief. But still, Levi couldn't imagine being loved that way, knew too well that he hadn't been in his past relationship.

But Adriana had a huge capacity for love. That was something else he'd learned over the last few days.

And Levi, despite his hesitations, all the reasons he knew it was a bad idea, still wondered what it would be like to be loved that much.

He sat in the driver's seat while Adriana and Mrs. Marston talked, then watched as the couple waved and Adriana walked to the car. She climbed in. He tried to keep his tone light as he navigated down the hill. "You up for a trip to the Raven's Rest coffee shop? I can drop you at your house if you need me to, and get someone there to watch you."

She looked near her breaking point and Levi didn't want to be responsible for her breaking.

"I'm not fragile, Levi. I can handle working this with you, okay? Let's go to the shop. But let's go home and get Blue."

He raised his eyebrows. "We're not looking for..."

"She's also a regular search dog. And the fact that we aren't looking for bodies today will make it so she doesn't need a break. Searching for the scent of someone who was living doesn't put as much strain on them." Adriana held up a pair of worn socks. "These were their daughter's. She wanted to give them to me, just in case I could figure more out from using them with Blue. Where Raina was taken from, why, anything like that. It's not too late to search for evidence of where she might have been."

Levi nodded.

"That makes sense. Okay, home to get your dog?" he asked.

Adriana nodded. "And then to the coffee shop."

Something in her voice was determined. Dark.

And he wondered, was she doing this only to get closure for the families affected by the serial killer and to ensure no one else died? Or was she somehow trying to get closure for herself as well?

Making cases personal was never a good way to handle things. He'd seen officers break down mentally because they took on the emotions of victims' families and got too close to situations. Compassion was important, but so was some distance.

He only hoped he could help Adriana avoid those mistakes.

"I'll be right back out," Adriana promised, leaving Levi alone in the car once they returned to her house. Her heart was pounding in her chest, much too rapidly to be normal, and she felt her hands beginning to sweat.

She'd had one panic attack in front of

Levi already. She certainly wasn't planning to have another.

Good thing she legitimately needed to . get her dog for this next job.

The house was empty, except for Babe and Blue, who both met her at the door. Adriana had felt some hesitation about coming inside alone, but even though Levi had offered to clear it for her and walk from room to room and confirm that the house was empty, she'd turned him down. If he came inside to check the house, he'd want to wait for her to gather what she needed and get ready, and she needed to be alone. To think.

She went through the motions of getting Blue ready. Grabbed a snack and a treat for later. Picked up the bag that held her SAR-K9 vest to put on her later as identification. Gave her some water in case she wanted one more drink before they left, though she had a portable bowl as well. Really, it was a stalling tactic to give herself a little more space from Levi and his gaze that seemed to see through to her soul. She need a little more time to try to breathe and calm herself down.

But it was like someone was gripping her chest with a vise and no matter how much she struggled, Adriana couldn't quite breathe.

She couldn't get over the attitude of the Marstons. Why hadn't they hated her and Levi for not being able to give them answers? While they shouldn't hate them, she knew all too well that grief turned sadness into anger in strange ways.

Hadn't she spent days, weeks after Robert's death blaming the rescue workers? Wondering whether, if they'd gotten there earlier, they could have helped?

Hating how calm they had seemed when her whole world had fallen apart? Maybe that was why she got so invested—too invested, according to Levi.

But they hadn't seemed affected by any of those negative emotions toward her or Levi. They'd been kind. Concerned about her safety.

Your daughter is dead. She'd kept thinking in her mind. *Your daughter is dead and you're worried about me?*

How did they move on? How did they keep caring about other people after what must be one of the worst losses, the most devastating?

No matter how hard she tried to swallow normally, slow down her heart rate, she couldn't. Finally, Adriana sank to the ground on the floor of her kitchen and leaned her head back against the pantry door.

In her pocket, her phone started buzzing. Adriana took another breath, then another, and finally decided to check it.

It was her SAR colleague Ellie.

Adriana considered, and then answered. "Hello?"

"Hey. Are you doing okay?"

How could she ask that question? Had Levi called her?

"Did Levi ask you to check on me?" she asked.

"No, but I was curious about that, too. I

heard you're working with him right now. How's that going? We miss you here."

Ellie's voice was normal, completely free of pity, and if Adriana didn't know better…well, it really did look like no one had told her to call.

Adriana glanced up at the ceiling, seeing in her mind's eye the heavens. Did God prompt people to make phone calls? Ellie was one of the people she could trust. And here her friend was, offering to talk to her.

She was past pride at this point, as nausea had crept in to join a variety of symptoms. "I'm not great," she admitted, her voice wavering.

"Is it Levi? I know he's always driven you crazy."

He had, hadn't he? But, no, working with Levi had been fine. It was her. Only her.

"I can't… I don't…" She struggled for breath. "All those people, Ellie. All those people I've been thinking about, that I'm supposed to be helping him find, they were murdered. And it's different than SAR work."

Her friend was quiet for a minute and Adriana worried she'd crossed some invisible line.

"That would be different. Do you want to talk more about it?" Ellie's voice was soft. Not demanding. Even though they were in different places, Adriana felt like Ellie was sitting next to her.

In that moment, Adriana felt like she wasn't alone. Her next breath came easier and she felt some of the pressure on her chest ease.

"I just don't know what to do. I don't know how to handle this."

"Have you told Levi? I'm sure he won't hold you to helping."

He wouldn't, she knew. He'd let her walk away right now. But Adriana didn't want that. She wasn't a quitter.

Yes, she'd walked away from her entire life near Anchorage years ago and started over here in Raven Pass, but that hadn't been about running away.

Or had it?

"I don't want to do that," she admitted. "I want him to see me as strong."

Ellie was quiet. Adriana heard her own words, felt a question rising in her own mind.

Then Ellie asked it aloud. "Are you...? Do you have feelings for him? You don't sound like this is just an obligation to a sometime coworker."

She didn't. Even to herself. Adriana couldn't argue. She thought about watching Levi work a case, about the way his green eyes weren't always playful as she'd once thought. He lightened up life, that was true, but when he was focused, he gave all his attention to his job. He was actually one of the most driven people she'd ever met and she'd never realized it before.

A tear fell down her face as she felt her shoulders relaxing.

Yes, she had feelings for him.

"You don't have to answer," Ellie said. "But if you did..."

Adriana waited.

"It would be okay. And you wouldn't have to hide those from him. And Adriana?"

Still, she didn't say anything back. Ellie didn't seem deterred. "I will talk to you whenever. I know we haven't always been super close, but you've always been one of the people here that I trust and I hope you feel the same."

"I do," she assured her friend.

"But," Ellie continued, "I think you can trust Levi with your anxiety, too. He won't see you as weak. If anything, he'll see how strong you are for not quitting."

It was something to consider.

The idea of relaxing, of telling him how she really felt about this case, instead of trying to wear a face of unbreakable confidence, reassured her.

Adriana blew out a breath, wiped one more tear. And felt her heartbeat return to normal as the tension in her shoulders dissipated.

"I'll try," she promised her friend.

"Good. You can trust him. He's a good man."

He was, Adriana knew, as she said goodbye and hung up. But the problem wasn't Levi. It was the idea that if she grew closer to him, then she'd be opening herself up to getting hurt again.

Losing someone she loved had almost destroyed her the last time. She couldn't do it again.

Still conflicted, she petted Blue one more time, then stood up and walked back outside, all evidence of what had just happened hopefully missing from her face.

"Everything okay?" Levi asked when Adriana opened the car door and climbed back inside.

She nodded. "Yes. It is now."

He looked at her. She waited for him to put the key in the ignition and head to the coffee shop where Raina had likely gone the afternoon of her death, but he didn't. Instead he just watched her.

Yes, she had to admit to herself as his

green eyes searched hers. She felt something for him. More than friendship.

She offered a small smile, tried to find a scrap of bravery. "This is hard," she admitted. "It's hard to see how lives have been destroyed. It's hard knowing that no matter how hard Blue and I work, we aren't going to be able to give any of these people back to those who loved them. They are all gone. And they were all murdered."

Instead of being concerned, or making a big deal out of the fact that she was half admitting to having a meltdown, he just nodded. With that came a sense of connection. To Levi. Because he responded the way she hadn't even realized she wanted him to—just acknowledgement.

"It is hard," he said. And then he put the car in Reverse and backed out of her driveway. Then drove toward the coffee shop.

Raven's Rest was typical of an Alaskan mountain-town coffee shop. Woodsy, with lots of log and wood architectural details, but with quirky local artwork.

That aesthetic usually made Adriana smile, but today she was having to wrestle with the idea that cheery places like this could have been related to something so depressing.

Life was like that. Good and bad, high and low, all mixed together. Alaska itself often reminded her of those kinds of contradictions of life. Beautiful and dangerous at the same time. God was the same even when either extreme was happening in life. That was something else she was learning, slowly.

She and Blue were standing outside the shop now, Levi with them. She'd told him he should just go in by himself to ask for information, while she let Blue smell around outside. Sometimes people watching her work made her nervous, and since her realization earlier today of the slight…attraction she had toward him, Levi watching her wouldn't help.

"I'm not leaving you out here alone. At the last place we think a murder victim was seen? Yeah, no."

Why abduct women from coffee shops? Did the killer hang out at these places often and were they just where he saw potential victims?

Or was it more than that?

She'd stayed up researching last night, serial killers in particular, and had learned more than she'd ever wanted to about them. Their habits still didn't make sense to her—which was good since by definition they were not normal, clear-thinking people—but they generally followed a pattern. Their killings weren't completely random, not in their twisted minds.

The coffee-shop element had to factor in somehow.

"Different coffee shops, right?" She turned to Levi.

"What?" He looked at her. He'd been studying the shop, like the storefront held the answers he needed.

"They haven't all been this one." She didn't think so. Surely he'd have mentioned that.

He shook his head. "None have been

here. Two were in the same coffee shop, but it doesn't appear there's any pattern with which shop or how often. Just that it's a coffee shop."

So not a location issue.

It still didn't make sense to her.

"We can both go in. This is Raven Pass. No one is going to bat an eye at a dog in a shop."

Maybe he was right. Alaska was extremely canine friendly, especially in quirky mountain towns of just a couple thousand people, like Raven Pass and neighboring Girdwood. But there was a difference between a standard-size dog and her sixty-pound Alaskan husky, which many people told her looked like a wolf.

Tall and rangy, with pointed ears and varying shades of creamy white and gray…

Yeah, she could see their point.

"You think no one is going to bat an eye at *her*?" Adriana raised her eyebrows and glanced down at her dog, who sat obediently at the end of her leash, looking for all the world like a sweetheart and not like an animal who'd just that morning stolen an entire cucumber off the kitchen counter and eaten it.

"If they do, we'll leave. Come on." Levi reached for the heavy wooden door, with its carved wooden handle, and held it open for her. Reluctantly, she walked inside, pausing for him to follow her once she'd stepped in.

The room was large, with high ceilings that sloped up toward the apex of the roof. At one end, a fire roared in a hearth beneath a mantel that spoke of warmth and made her want to cuddle up in one of the chairs near it, maybe with a blanket.

In front of the entrance was the bar area, with a pastry display case.

Oh, those looked really good.

Maybe this shop would help her get her appetite back. It had been somewhat absent since the awkward conversations with the Marstons and her growing...awareness of Levi.

If anything could, it was the blueberry

crumble in the pastry case right there. Or the chocolate-chip banana buckwheat muffin.

"Hi, can I help you?" The woman at the counter had long dark hair and looked to be in her midtwenties. She was gorgeous, Adriana noted and looked over at Levi without meaning to.

Though why, she didn't know. Even if she was developing a slight...crush or something on him, it was still silly. She had no claim on him. None whatsoever. They were *barely* more than coworkers, probably not even that. She needed to remember the way he'd pulled his hand away from her, and the way he'd backed off after realizing a question he'd asked had been personal the other day—

Everything about their interactions made it clear he wasn't looking to get to know her. Her own feelings were something she could deal with. And she could trust him enough to share her anxiety struggles—she thought Ellie was right about that.

But that was different than making him aware of her feelings about him.

She needed to try to ignore how she felt about him. *However* that was. She didn't want to think too hard about it.

Levi smiled at the woman at the counter, but with his regular, normal amount of warmth. "Hi."

The woman looked disappointed. At least it wasn't just Adriana who couldn't catch his attention.

"We have a couple of questions about a woman who was here earlier this week," he said.

The barista's eyebrows raised. "We get a lot of people in here."

"This was a woman, blonde. Raina Marston." Levi held up his phone, which had a picture of her on the screen. It was a picture from social media, Adriana could see. He must have saved it when he'd been looking at her profiles earlier.

"She's come in before. I don't know when, though." The woman shrugged, looking at least a little apologetic. "Like I said, we're busy."

"Can you try to remember the last time she came in?" Levi asked it in a much nicer voice than Adriana would have. It was taking all the self-control she possessed to stay quiet when this employee clearly didn't feel compelled to help them.

"I think it was Tuesday. I remember seeing her in here talking to a man." She frowned. Then opened a drawer and shuffled through a binder.

"Nathan Hall." She pointed at a receipt. "I remembered because he was really cute and I was thinking if she didn't go out with him again I sure would." She shrugged.

So Raina had met a man here, someone she might have been dating.

And then Raina had never been seen by anyone again. But that accounted for at least part of the missing hours they had.

And there was a man involved. Interesting.

"Thanks so much for your time." Levi

smiled again. "Could we get a couple of lattes to go also?"

They stood in silence while the woman made them and then handed one to each of them. Levi paid.

"Thanks," Adriana said. The two of them walked back out of the shop.

"Well?" Levi turned to Adriana as soon as they were outside.

"'Well' what?" she asked and then took a sip of her latte. She was usually a caramel macchiato sort of girl, but this was nice. Sweeter than she thought, with just espresso and milk.

She glanced at Levi. *Huh.*

"What did you think?"

Levi had made it pretty clear he was going to treat her like an actual partner. She may as well just take a deep breath and do her best to swim. She'd been tossed in the deep end of this investigation, so it was that or sink.

Adriana was tired, so very tired, of letting herself sink.

"I think it's strange she met a man here

and no one knew. No best friend noticed? She hadn't mentioned him?"

"Online dating, maybe?"

Adriana shrugged. "Possibly."

"Let's go find Nathan Hall," Levi said, heading for the car.

"Wait." Adriana found the nerve to interrupt, since they'd brought Blue all the way out here and the dog hadn't even gotten a cup of whipped cream for her troubles. That was probably okay, since too much dairy wasn't good for dogs, but Adriana didn't want the trip out to be for nothing. Blue was wearing her vest, so she knew she was working, or would be soon. "I still need to look around. As long as we're here, let me give Blue the scent and see if she picks anything up on the trails right here." Adriana nodded to the woods next to the coffee shop, which had trails running through them. "That way we would at least know if whoever took her did so by car or walked her into the woods."

It made sense to go ahead and check, Levi thought.

"You're right." Levi stopped. Nodded. "Okay, let's do that, then."

Adriana petted Blue for a minute, then reached down with the socks.

"Ready, girl?"

TEN

Once again, to Levi it looked almost like magic, how the dog and her owner worked together. Or maybe his thoughts were just clouded by the fact that Adriana herself looked like magic. Her eyes were sparkling, and he could tell she loved this part of her job—the search, her dog as a partner—and her hair was in loose curls around her shoulders, dark and shining in the sunshine.

He was supposed to be getting her help with this investigation, not noticing her hair, her curls, or the way she looked at life. But he kept finding himself distracted.

Not enough that he felt it interfered with his investigation. But he did need her. He just had to let her help and somehow keep his emotions in check, hold her at arm's length, and that was getting harder to do.

He'd actually grabbed her hand that morning. He remembered how it felt under his. Warm. Soft. And then he remembered the exact moment he'd realized what he was doing, that he couldn't do that, and had yanked it away.

She'd looked almost hurt, just before her face had become unreadable, but surely...

So maybe she was attracted to him, too. In that case, it was just a mutual case of "what a bad idea." A cop and an SAR worker? Not exactly a perfect match. Twice the stress, twice the danger, twice the heaviness. Levi needed to find a sweet...preschool teacher or something. Someone who didn't snark at him, who didn't make him feel so...

Alive. Because when someone made you feel alive like that, and then they left?

Yeah, he knew what that was like. Although had Melissa ever made him feel quite like Adriana did? He honestly wasn't sure.

Either way, the way he was drawn to her wasn't something he should act on, he knew that. He wasn't ready to try again with love. Not yet. Maybe he never would be.

Because even though he knew he hadn't been to blame for all that had gone wrong in their relationship, part of him still wondered… What if it was him? What if he wasn't a good enough husband?

What if he tried again, fell in love with Adriana and then wasn't enough for her?

No. He definitely wasn't ready.

He followed her into the woods after she'd given Blue the scent from the article of clothing the Marstons had given her.

"The idea is that she'll get the scent and I'll be able to tell from her behavior if Raina was here, and if she was taken deeper into the woods or not," Adriana explained.

Levi just nodded and tried to keep up as Blue walked on one of the established trails. Raven Pass was crisscrossed with them. Many of them became ski trails in the winter and he thought this might be one of them, with how wide it was. There was plenty of room to walk beside Adriana, so he did.

He sensibly resisted the urge to grab her hand.

Besides, she was working right now. She wouldn't want that.

Then again, he didn't know *what* she wanted. He'd studiously avoided any kind of conversation that could get too serious or make them feel too close to each other.

Because the fact was he just couldn't take getting hurt again. And Adriana was so *much*. In a good way. So much sunshine. So much fire. Spark. So much potential to break his heart and he just couldn't do that again. Not right now.

"She was here." Adriana said it quietly. "Somewhere near here."

"You can tell that?"

She shrugged. "Technically, not for sure. Blue hasn't alerted. There's nothing objective to say that I'm right. But from knowing my dog, I would say yes."

Levi nodded. "Anything more solid than that? Should we keep looking?"

Adriana shrugged. "Give me a bit longer, but I'm thinking no." She turned around, made her way back toward the parking lot, watching the dog's behavior carefully.

"I think she gets the scent almost just as strongly out there. Now you'll understand this is my interpretation, but I think probably it's just that the scent got trapped in the trees. I don't think she was ever in the woods. I think she was probably only here in the parking lot."

Levi stepped a few steps away and looked around. It was easy to imagine the day much like this one. Some cars in the parking lot.

"If she didn't leave the parking lot on her own, then our best course of action is to find the guy she was with."

"Did she mention him to friends? On social media?" Adriana asked.

"Friends have been interviewed and didn't mention anything. Officer Koser conducted those earlier today and texted me to say that nothing new turned up. Social media didn't have anything definitive either."

"Wouldn't she have mentioned him to her parents? If she'd been meeting him?" Levi raised his eyebrows. "So you think she met him and he took her?"

Levi shook his head. "No."

"No?" She waited.

"Did you hear what the barista *didn't* say?" Levi asked as he opened the car door.

She opened hers while she thought and let Blue climb in first.

Adriana had just started to shake her head when he continued.

"The barista didn't mention their meeting being strange. If this is the same killer who began committing crimes more than twenty years ago, he couldn't meet with a woman that young without sticking out. See what I mean? The killer has to be years older. The cashier at the coffee shop would have been more specific, about her meeting an older man. And unless it was Harrison Ford's doppelgänger, she wouldn't have made the comment about him being handsome."

All of which made sense. SAR puzzles just made so much more sense to her than the law-enforcement kind. Not for the first time, she couldn't help but think how eager she was for this case to be over, to get back to her normal job.

Although she wouldn't see Levi as often. Although their paths crossed on occasion, it would be a rare occurrence. Not every day.

She would miss him, she realized. Which made her aware of another truth. Even if they were only friends, it would still hurt her if he disappeared from her life.

Was there no way to protect herself from all possible pain?

Please don't let me get hurt, she prayed, while trying to focus on the task at hand.

"So who is the guy?" she asked.

"No idea," Levi admitted as he put the car in Reverse. "But hopefully that's what we're going to find out. Let's go to the police department, get his address and then go talk to him."

At Adriana's request, they dropped off Blue at her place on their way to the police department. While they were there, Adriana offered to fix some lunch for them. Her stomach had started growling earlier and she was sure he must be hungry, too.

"No, it's fine. You don't need to do that."

"I'm happy to." She was already halfway through the assembly of two roast-beef sandwiches. Each of her dogs had also had a tiny piece of roast beef, even though they couldn't have much since the sodium wasn't good for them. A little for a treat was okay, though.

"I just feel bad. It's not your job to feed me."

And yet, packing two lunches felt so good to her. It was nice to consider someone besides herself and to feel like she was helping to take care of him.

Had he had a previous girlfriend make him feel bad for requesting that she make him food? Or something similar? Even as she thought it, Adriana was surprised at how much she disliked the concept of him ever having had a significant other. Of course, he would have, though. Men as handsome as Levi didn't stay single their entire lives.

"Why are you being so weird about this?" She finally couldn't hold back the words, even knowing it wasn't really her business.

He seemed comfortable around her. Comfortable in her house, sitting at her table with coffee. He was personable, at least on a professional level.

But there was some kind of line he'd drawn in invisible sand that he wouldn't let himself cross.

Of all things, *that* should make her back off. Leave him alone.

But some flash of insecurity in his kind, light eyes had her feeling like whatever the line was about, it wasn't what he really wanted.

He was looking at her now, hesitation in his gaze.

She stepped closer. Handed him the bag with his lunch in it. "Here."

He nodded and took it from her. "Thank you."

She made herself step back. The last thing she wanted to do was jeopardize their working relationship.

"Ready?" he asked. She nodded and followed him outside onto her front deck.

Maybe she'd been right. Maybe making lunch was too personal a thing.

She turned to lock her door, then opened her mouth to apologize as Levi, who was standing beside her, held his remote up to unlock his patrol car.

The car exploded in a concussive blast, the fireball sending out a wall of force that punched and pushed them backward.

Adriana stumbled back, or flew, she couldn't tell. Or had Levi shoved her? They landed hard on the wooden deck, and Adriana could feel a bruise forming on her hip where she'd taken most of the impact. Her ears were still ringing from the blast and a thrumming headache had started pounding.

For a second she was lying there, her mind trying to grapple with what had happened and make it make sense. But there wasn't much chance of that. Nothing about this made sense.

"Book inside, now. The house." Levi's breathless voice beside her left no room to argue.

She scrambled behind her for the doorknob, scooting back toward the house for safety.

Her keys. Where were her keys?

The car in the driveway was still burning, a creaking, crackling heap of useless metal.

She had been in that vehicle half an hour ago. So had her dog.

Keys. She had to focus on getting inside. She blinked away a fresh wave of dizziness and fumbled across the front deck on her hands and knees.

There they were.

She reached for them and unlocked the door. "Come with me," she said to Levi and surprisingly, he didn't argue.

They both stepped into the house. Both dogs were barking, dancing in a frenzy of excitement. Adriana almost couldn't breathe. They'd almost been killed.

Incinerated.

No.

"What happened?" she finally asked, her heartbeat still in a tangle in her chest.

His face didn't reassure her. For once, his expression said nothing about having this under control, and only hinted at confusion.

Even fear…

"Someone is taking this awfully far." At least that's what she thought he mumbled. It was hard to hear, from the way he clenched his teeth.

"Should I call 911?" The words felt silly.

A cop was standing here with her and he hadn't been able to stop the attack.

"Yes," he said, again surprising her. He held up his phone, which was vibrating. "I'm sorry, I have to take this."

If he could ignore the look on Adriana's face and just do his job, Levi knew he'd have a much better chance at solving this case.

"Hello?" he said into the phone as he walked away from her, despite the look of sheer, unmasked fear in her wide eyes.

There was no answering voice at the other end. But the "unknown number" on his caller ID had made him ready for anything. Expecting anything.

"Officer Wicks."

Prepared or not, it was still spine-chilling to hear his name uttered by a genderless, heavily computerized voice.

"This isn't your fight. You don't have all the information. It is necessary to do this. Stop getting in the way. Next time, the bomb goes off with you in the car."

He fumbled in his pocket for a piece of paper, to write down the caller's words. But, of course, he had none when he needed it.

The phone clicked. No more voice. No more words.

"I called it in." Adriana walked toward him, her voice shaking. "Who was that?"

"I need paper." He ignored her question for now, trying to focus on what had been said to him. "Do you have some?"

Her eyes widened even more at his short tone. He would apologize later, but not right now. Right now he needed to write down the message as best he could remember it.

"What on earth?" Adriana muttered under her breath as she handed him the paper. Levi scrawled down the message, knowing he was forgetting some of the word choices and hoping he was close enough.

The part that had stuck with him most was the fact that the caller—theoretically, the serial killer he was after—felt justified in his or her actions. Not that it surprised him. Serial killers often felt they were righting some kind of perceived wrong, or helping the world in some way, according to their warped perspectives. But this person's words hadn't sounded crazy, which was perhaps the creepiest thing about the call.

He'd been on the phone with a person who had killed over five people. That person was now after *him*.

It was more than he wanted to grapple with right now. Especially with his shell of a patrol car burning in the driveway.

"The caller said next time I'd be inside," he mumbled. That implied that his unlocking the door hadn't set off the mechanism of the bomb, as he'd assumed. Instead, someone had chosen when to remotely trigger it.

The killer apparently had triggered it right when they were close enough to be in real danger, to have *almost* died.

"Why does this person appear to keep halfheartedly attempting to kill me?"

"Because they don't have the same kind of compulsion to kill you as they do the other victims." He heard Judah's voice as his brother stepped inside the front door, which Adriana had apparently left open. "You really should shut that. The fire department is outside putting the fire out, but that doesn't mean leaving the door unlocked is a good plan with a serial killer."

Levi hadn't meant to ask the question aloud, but nodded at his brother anyway. "Thanks for letting me know. Didn't mean to leave it unlocked. So tell me what you think of this—the killer keeps doing things that might kill me, but doesn't try too hard because he'd rather I just back off?"

Judah nodded. "Exactly. You are in the way of whatever his plan is. But you aren't one of the ones who is 'supposed' to die, according to him."

It was a sick train of thought to consider. But it made sense.

The problem for him was that he wasn't

going to quit. Which meant he would stay in the way and still be in danger.

And the more Adriana pitched in on the case, the more she would be in danger, too. Because the killer didn't have anything against him personally. He was just a liability. And she was, too, now that she was helping. Serial killers, while they murdered people who fit their profile, also were known to kill people who didn't fit the profile but who got in their way. Like law enforcement.

And, he feared in this case, like search-and-rescue workers who had volunteered to help with the case and had the skills to blow it wide open.

"I came as soon as we got the call." Judah was speaking to him again. Then he turned to Adriana. "Thanks for calling it in. You did a good job giving details and staying calm. The dispatch worker was impressed with that."

Adriana offered a small smile and Levi felt proud of her. That was weird, wasn't it, like they were something more than friends?

"Thanks. I didn't feel that calm, but I've learned in SAR work that panic doesn't get you anywhere," Adriana said from where she stood petting her dogs. Blue had barked when they'd come inside, but almost seemed to sense that Adriana needed her to be calm now. Both Blue and Babe stood by her like sentries, letting her pet them.

"The killer called me," Levi said, wondering if he should have waited until Adriana had left the room to tell his brother.

"And said?" Judah asked.

Adriana asked nothing. She just stared, eyes wide.

"Essentially warned me that next time I'd be in the car." Levi showed Judah and Adriana the words he'd jotted down.

"Give me the phone number it came from?"

"Blocked." Levi shook his head.

"Not that hard to do these days," Judah said.

"So he's trying to give you a chance to live by stopping the investigation," Adriana chimed in. "And you can't take it because it would mean other people dying."

Well, when she put it that way, he sounded like some kind of hero, and if he was honest with himself, he saw a spark of something in her eye that seemed to imply she almost thought of him that way, too.

But she couldn't, surely. She must see the way that he worked too much, like his wife had said. And the way he tended to be a bit of a lone wolf. He'd worked well with Jim in the past, but he got tired of waiting for other people sometimes and preferred to just charge ahead alone when he had an idea. All of those things made him imperfect and she was *still* looking at him that way.

He didn't deserve it. And somehow never wanted it to stop.

When this case was solved, what was he going to do? Adriana would still be a coworker, so not anyone he could afford to casually date, lest they break each other's heart and make their jobs awkward.

But he'd gotten so used to having her at his side during the course of these last few days that he would miss her.

Maybe more than as just a listening ear. If he let himself, he could admit that he enjoyed spending time with her just as a person, as a woman, which was something he hadn't let himself feel in years.

"You must be getting uncomfortably close," Judah offered, "for the killer to be willing to escalate things this way."

"Or they are just getting unhinged." Adriana didn't look pleased with that idea.

Levi couldn't say he was, either. And Judah's tightened jaw spoke for itself.

"I've got guys outside ready to look at the car when it's cool enough," Judah said finally. "To see what type of bomb it was and if there is any kind of forensic evidence that could help us out."

"Are you expecting to find any?" Adriana asked.

"Not really," Judah admitted. "Not eas-

ily, anyway. Whoever this is has been killing for years. They could get sloppy. But
only if they're desperate."

"I like the idea of someone getting desperate enough to leave evidence, but not
enough to actually want them after me
like that," Levi said, attempting a joke.

His brother, as he should have known
would be the case, was not amused.

"Is this some kind of joke to you?" Judah's voice lowered and his tone darkened. "That your car got blown up, the
first Raven Pass cruiser ever to be destroyed—by the way, I heard that tidbit
from Officer Clark on the way here—
and that someone is after you? That's just
funny?"

"I'm going to go make sure Blue got
enough food earlier." Adriana cleared her
throat.

Great. They'd made her feel awkward in
her own house. That was another level of
being a bad guest. Bad enough that she'd
made him lunch today, like it was her job
to take care of him.

No one had taken care of him since the day he'd moved out of his house after high-school graduation. No one. Not like that.

It still stung that the marriage he'd thought might have that kind of love hadn't. No, instead it had only left him with betrayal from the discovery of her unfaithfulness and a deep sense of cynicism that he couldn't shake no matter how lighthearted he tried to be about life.

And rather than thank Adriana for the sandwich, for thinking of him, and actually find the guts to tell her why he'd acted so weird, he'd gotten his car blown up in her driveway and interrupted her safe world with this entire case.

Yeah, he might miss her when this was all over, but she would undoubtedly be glad to be rid of him.

"Of course I don't think it's funny," he said now to his brother, doing the best he could to keep some of the pure anger from his tone. Judah was still his brother, no matter what kind of stupid things he might say sometimes. "I think it's awful and I want it to end—that's why I'm barely sleeping and I'm working this case every single second I'm awake."

"So don't make jokes."

"It's what I do, okay? Some people drink too much, some people find a hobby, some people make jokes to handle it. Let me do things my way."

Judah stared at him in that way only older brothers could, and then Levi really heard himself.

"Yeah, okay, I could make jokes and also handle it better, too. Pray about it? Is that what you're thinking?"

Sometimes Judah was a lot like their eldest brother, Ryan, that way. Levi followed Jesus, too—at least he sure tried his best—but it had never been quite the same for him as it was for his two older brothers. For all his gruff attitude, Judah loved Jesus in a big way, the same with Ryan.

Levi…followed Him. Knew a lot about Him. And had trusted Him to save him.

He loved Him. Sure. Just not, you know, in a squishy, overly emotional kind of way.

Something that was hardly Judah's business. He didn't care what his brother thought, or that he might disagree.

"Let me handle my life, Judah," he said, and pain flashed in Judah's eyes.

"Fine," his brother said and walked away.

ELEVEN

She wasn't trying to eavesdrop, truly she wasn't, but Adriana could hear every word from the kitchen. Neither of the brothers were trying particularly hard to be quiet.

It made her uncomfortable beyond belief that the killer had probably called Levi. It was even worse knowing that the person had insinuated that the bomb had been triggered remotely, which meant someone had to have been watching them.

She looked around the house, where she'd always felt so comfortable, and ran her eyes over the ceilings, down the walls. Looked at the room full of furniture.

Were they listening, too? Surely her house hadn't been compromised. No one could have gotten inside without the dogs alerting her to it.

Right?

"Sorry you had to hear that," Levi said as he walked into the kitchen and sighed. The sound came from deep within, less frustration and more heaviness. "I assume you did, based on the fact that you're just standing here, looking alarmed."

She was literally caught in the act. Adriana felt her face color, but she shrugged, refusing to feel bad for overhearing a conversation that had taken place in her own house.

"You guys will work it out. Families do that." TV made it seem like that, anyway. Her family fought and threatened and stormed out. Her parents had divorced when she was two. Her siblings had more drama in their lives than a daytime TV show. So she didn't know from experience. But deep down, Judah and Levi both seemed to care too much about each other not to want to patch up their differences. She suspected faith made an impact on that. She was the only Christian in her own family, and while it certainly didn't make her perfect, it did make her want to live her life a certain way, to be at peace with other people.

"We'll see. He's gone outside to keep an eye on the scene until more officers get here. Right now I'm more worried about who blew up my car."

His voice was more gruff than usual, a low, gravelly growl. He was taking this personally and she understood and didn't blame him.

Someone had crossed a line today. Several lines.

"What now?" she asked him, watching his expression as he thought about her question.

His facial muscles relaxed, and Adriana felt relieved that she'd said the right thing.

"When they finish looking at my car, we're going to look at the list of known victims in this case and try to figure out why the killer feels like he or she is justified."

Not what she'd expected. "What?"

"Whoever is after me seems to think he is doing some kind of service. It's a mission to rid the world of people doing something wrong."

"That sweet woman you looked up on social media, that we heard her parents talk about for hours?" Adriana shook her head.

Levi shrugged. "Listen, I'm not judging any of the victims. Obviously, no one actually deserved to die and our killer is absolutely crazy. But people aren't what they seem. You get used to that, especially working in the job that I do."

Maybe that explained his cynicism. Still, Adriana felt like it must have more to do with a past relationship than just cases Levi had worked. He held on to his hesitation to trust too tightly for it to be just work related.

At least she thought so. Would she ever have the chance to ask him about it?

The memory of his hand on her flitted

across her brain, entirely inappropriate to the situation, and she swatted it away.

"Are we going to talk to Nathan Hall, the man who was having coffee with Raina?" Adriana asked because she felt like they were jumping around. In SAR work, she didn't just leave the search grid and run off to someone else's unless she had an exceptionally concrete reason to do so.

Nothing the caller had said to Levi sounded like that kind of reason to her. No, it felt like they should stay focused on what they had been doing before.

He stared at her for a minute, and the hard planes of his jaw showed no hint of softening into a smile. For a second, she wished she hadn't offered her thoughts at all. After all, as she kept reminding herself, she wasn't an equal partner in this. She was a K9 handler, a small aspect of the case, and for Levi to involve her in any more than that was giving her a glimpse into a world and a case where she didn't fully belong. He was the one who had the training and knew what he was doing. She needed to trust him to do it.

"You're right." He nodded once. "Let's eat some food and go talk to that guy. You're right, that's where we should have started."

Their sandwiches were still in the bags on the front deck, but going outside to retrieve them would have done nothing for Adriana's appetite, so she remade them, offering Levi one and biting into the other.

"I'll let you buy me ice cream for dessert after we talk to him," she said around bites, still uneasy with how serious Levi was being. She had truly misjudged him. If anything, he was *too* focused when working a case. He didn't take anything lightly at all.

Why did she insist on assuming things about people she didn't know? It was a bad habit she needed to break.

"That sounds like a good plan."

There, she'd almost gotten a smile from him. It was enough for now. She finished her sandwich. Levi had finished before her and was already getting ready to leave.

"Would you mind if we took your car?" he asked her.

Adriana smiled. "I had assumed."

"Someone is dropping off another patrol car for me later. But they're not here yet, clearly. Before we go anywhere—" his voice had no hint of humor and neither did his face "—I want the crime scene team to check your car for us and make sure there's nothing...wrong."

Interesting, roundabout way to say that he wanted them to make sure there wasn't a bomb inside it anywhere, but in some ways she could appreciate him not wanting to say that out loud.

She didn't particularly want to articulate those thoughts, either.

More officers arrived soon, including the crime-scene team Levi had mentioned. Their check of her car revealed that it was fine. Adriana hesitated before they left, trying to decide whether it was safer for the dogs to stay or come with them, but in the end she decided that law enforcement would probably have a presence outside her house for most of the time they were gone.

"Smart choice," Levi told her when they were finally driving away. The shell of his car still sat in the driveway. "They'll be safe there."

Adriana hoped so. While it was no secret to anyone who knew her how much she loved her dogs, she doubted her friends fully realized that the animals were all she had left.

Yes, technically her mother was still alive. But her being in prison didn't exactly lend itself to a close relationship. Adriana thought she might have a sister in there, too, at this point.

If anyone understood her family situation, they'd know multiple things about her. First, why she'd so willingly followed Robert up to Alaska. Second, why her dogs meant the world to her.

That was what happened when the people you should have been able to count on in life couldn't be counted on for anything.

"So did you get Nathan Hall's address?"

Levi had left her alone before they'd left her house and had gone outside to talk to his fellow officers.

"Yes, we were able to call the station and they looked it up for me."

"Was he in your system?"

"He had a parking ticket a couple of years ago. But mostly they know how to research online." He smiled at her, the first real smile she'd seen of his in what felt like hours.

How long had it been since they'd been at the coffee shop? This day would not end.

"What did they find out?"

"He's twenty-nine, works on the north slope with an oil company two weeks on, two weeks off. Has a dating profile on at least one website," Levi said.

"Does he know we are coming?" She wasn't sure how cops did it in real life.

Did they show up unannounced, hoping to surprise people?

"He knows someone wants to talk to him, but not that we are coming now."

She nodded, trying to take it in. She hadn't had nearly enough time to think before they were pulling into a driveway of a nice house on Blueberry Street, one of the residential areas of Raven Pass, with twisty, narrow neighborhood roads and a lot of houses close together.

It wasn't the kind of place she pictured a serial killer living. But that didn't make Nathan Hall innocent.

"I should have brought Blue to sniff out the area, to see if Raina was ever here," she said, mostly thinking out loud. She climbed out of the car once Levi had parked and followed him to the front door.

"She wasn't here. Really. I think you're going to agree with me that he's not part of the equation at all when we are talking about the disappearance."

"So why are we talking to him?"

"He was likely the last person besides

the killer to see her alive. That counts for something. And a guy she was meeting for coffee—whether they met online like we wonder, or in some other way—might have some different kinds of insights than her parents had. I still want to figure out what the killer was saying on the phone when he said they 'deserved it,' or however he phrased it."

The words still gave Adriana chills, as did the fact that Levi had really talked to him in person at all.

"Okay, makes sense." She stood beside him at the door, waiting for him to ring the bell.

She wondered if the next half hour or so was going to give them another lead. And how close they'd be to a killer before this was all over.

Levi had beaten himself up all the way to Nathan Hall's house, even as he'd talked to Adriana and tried to seem relatively calm. He'd lost it, back there at the house. Something about seeing his car incinerated in Adriana's driveway and getting a threatening call inside her house...both had messed up his head.

Of course he needed to talk to Hall. This whole case had him so messed up, so out of order, that more than once he'd broken procedure and rather than go in a logical order, bounced around.

His panicked investigation wasn't going to help anyone. It could hurt. He needed to make this less personal, and fast.

Adriana was...

They were...

Yes, he wanted her to be safe. But he had to get her out of his head, had to get rid of this sense of urgency.

Deep breaths, solve the case. One logical step at a time. Like his brother would.

"Can I help you?"

The man who answered the door was a few inches taller than Levi. Average build, nice enough looking, he would guess, though he didn't really know what women considered attractive these days. In any case, there was nothing glaringly wrong with him that disproved their working theory about Raina having met him on an online-dating website.

"Officer Wicks, Raven Pass Police Department." Levi flashed his badge. "We have some questions for you about Raina Marston."

The man's face went pale.

"She never texted me back. Is she... okay?"

If he was acting, he deserved an award because Levi was familiar with the genuine signs of shock and he could see them all on this guy's features.

"Can I ask how you met her?" Levi ignored the question.

He named a popular online-dating site, not the one Levi's coworkers had found his profile on. Apparently he was a member of more than one.

Levi nodded, made a note to call the police department and have someone confirm his story later, that Raina had an account on that site.

"Is she okay?" Hall asked again.

This time Levi didn't ignore him. "I'm sorry, no. She was murdered and we need to ask you some questions. You may have been one of the last to see her alive."

His eyes widened and he nodded, stepping out of the doorway and back into the house just enough to motion them in. "Come inside, I'm happy to talk to you."

They stepped in.

"Have a seat." Nathan Hall motioned to the dining room table. They followed him and sat.

The first thing Levi noticed was the mess everywhere. Not a serious mess, like he'd seen in some child-abuse or drug cases he'd worked, but clutter. The house itself was nicely decorated.

Levi waited. "Is anyone else here we should talk to?"

"No, not right now... She's not... I don't..." Nathan Hall pulled at the collar of his shirt.

And bingo. He'd found what the man was hiding.

Adriana was looking around also, but

the slight frown on her face said she wasn't quite where he was yet in his thinking.

"So, to clarify, you have a…girlfriend who lives here also?"

Hall shook his head. "She doesn't… No one else lives here."

"No girlfriend?"

Maybe he'd pushed it one question too far, but the embarrassed man finally squared his shoulders and glared back at Levi.

"The decor is my wife's, okay? She isn't here because she left me. She isn't coming back."

And yet, the place mats on the table said the breakup must have been recent enough that the man probably shouldn't have been on an online dating site.

"You were just on a casual kind of date with Raina, right?" Adriana asked in a calm voice.

Levi almost cut her off. First of all, they didn't need to lead him to any kind of answer. Second, he couldn't believe the way she was talking to the guy. Like he was worth any kind of compassion. The guy had cheated on his wife. Levi had no sympathy for anyone who would do that.

No, it wasn't that. Everyone needed compassion. Years in law enforcement had convinced Levi of that and he was used to showing it to people who didn't seem to deserve it.

It was the fact that she seemed to have some sympathy toward him. Like she understood?

The only reason Levi was able to keep his own voice calm was that he knew that would put the suspect at ease, make him more likely to give them more information. It was basic police knowledge. Surely Adriana's casual lack of reaction was the same thing. She couldn't really understand that kind of thing. At least he hoped not. Sure, it was his business as a friend to hope she had better moral standards—at least that's what he told himself.

"Yes. Casual." Nathan's shoulders fell. "I didn't mean for her to get hurt."

His wife, or Raina?

Levi didn't say anything but Nathan met his eyes. "Either of them," he said and answered the question like it had been asked aloud.

"So did one of them find out about the other?" Again, Adriana's voice was soft. But now that Levi had calmed down he could hear the probing quality in it. She was trying to get information. The least he could do was be quiet and thank her later for doing his job for him.

Nathan shook his head. "Not as far as I know." He blew out a breath. "Yeah, well, maybe. I mean, my wife suspects—that's why she left—but..." He caught himself quickly. "She wouldn't. You don't think...?"

That his wife had tried to punish his sorry self by killing the woman he admitted to having one date in a coffee shop with? No. Besides, they were chasing a serial killer.

Adriana looked to Levi. He shook his head.

"Listen, ask me whatever you need to,

okay? But I want to get that part of my life over with and keep trying to work things out with my wife."

Considering it had been less than a week since Raina's disappearance, it seemed an awfully quick about-face of that lifestyle, but Levi reminded himself that deciding that really wasn't his problem.

"Did you know her before you saw one another at the coffee shop?"

Nathan shook his head. Then paused. "Well, sort of, yes. We met online. We had been text messaging back and forth for about a week. She'd asked if we could meet, but I was still deciding. The day we met for coffee, I had decided last-minute that I did want to meet. I sent her a text and she agreed to meet and suggested Raven's Rest."

It seemed consistent with her parents' story. If she'd been planning to get coffee that afternoon, anyway, then using that as a meeting place made sense also. Still. "Can we see the messages?"

The man reached in his pocket for his

phone, punched the screen a few times and handed it to Levi.

He read through them. Fairly standard. They felt closer than they were because they were talking online, they'd decided to finally meet…

Reading the messages sent chills up his spine. Not because there was anything strange about the messages, although it still bothered him to know that Nathan had sent them when he'd been married. It wasn't that he felt like he was perfect and got to sit on a throne and judge other people. But trust and faithfulness mattered to Levi. It hurt to know not everyone felt that way.

"Thanks." He handed the phone back to Nathan. It supported the story as he had told it.

The man wasn't full of integrity. But Levi doubted he was a killer. They'd keep him on a person-of-interest list out of an abundance of caution, warn him they might need to talk to him again, but he hadn't been an adult long enough to have been the one who'd committed the crimes decades ago.

It might not be someone from Raven Pass at all.

It might be time to pull in some guys from other agencies, maybe talk to the FBI in Anchorage about the situation. The last thing Levi wanted was to turn the case over to anyone else, but he also didn't want his pride and determination to get in the way of it being solved.

"Thanks for your time," he said as he stood. Adriana looked surprised but she stood as well. "We'll be back in touch. Don't leave the state without talking to someone."

His eyes widened. "I'm not like a suspect, right?"

"You're still part of the investigation."

Nathan's face fell but he nodded. "Okay, I hope you find out what happened. She seemed really sweet."

He'd been planning to see her again, hadn't he? Levi had to shake his head.

Levi opened the front door and held it

open for Adriana, who walked out in front of him.

They both eyed the car suspiciously, but what were they going to do? They had to drive it. Levi climbed underneath and gave the undercarriage a cursory once-over. Same with under the hood.

"You don't think…?" Adriana trailed off.

"We would have seen someone mess with it, the short amount of time we were in there."

At least he hoped so.

"It's fine." He paused. "You wait until I turn it on before you climb in, though, okay?"

She stepped back onto the front deck.

He started the car. Nothing happened.

She hurried and climbed in beside him. "I never should have let you do that. I didn't like that at all, thank you." Her voice was tight and tense.

"I didn't want to put you in danger."

She didn't comment, just stared at him, like maybe she didn't love the idea of him being in peril, either. Something was thick in the air between them and Levi waited, but Adriana didn't say anything. The look in her eyes, though...

Could he read women anymore? More importantly, could he read *this* woman? Because everything in her eyes said she cared about him. That maybe it would be more than professional courtesy to be upset if he'd blown up. And he had to admit that he cared about her, too.

He mattered to her. The thought was a weight on his chest. He had let someone down the last time they'd mattered to him. He must have, surely, or his wife wouldn't have been unfaithful, wouldn't have left him.

He could vaguely hear Ryan's voice in his head, disputing that. His family had told him it wasn't his fault. His pastor, too, had reassured him.

Still, some part of him repeated the lie like the echo of a beat on a bass drum.

Your fault. Your fault.

Adriana couldn't look at him that way. He didn't deserve it.

But unless he was wrong…she was. He looked away, tried to break whatever pull there was between them.

"What did you think?" she finally asked after a few minutes of neither of them speaking.

"About Nathan Hall?"

"Yes."

He shook his head. "I can't believe he'd do that to his wife or Raina. I couldn't stand to listen to him try to explain."

"Do you think he knows anything, though? About her disappearance?"

Levi shook his head.

"I agree." She hesitated. "On both counts. Did…? I mean… You know what, it's not my business, never mind."

"What?" he asked as he drove toward the police department. Since the trip to talk to Nathan had mostly been a bust, he wanted to pick up information about the other victims to take back to Adriana's house to work on. Of course, she didn't know that yet, but he was hoping she'd be okay with the plan.

He'd toyed with the idea of moving her to a safe house but knew she'd be resistant to that. Sure, they could work on the case at the police department, but she'd still have to go back to her house to sleep. They might as well work from there now. She wasn't less safe there than she was anywhere else. The attacks could have happened anywhere.

"Nothing."

Clearly it hadn't had anything to do with the case, so Levi let it go. It was surprising, though, that she'd think to ask what seemed like it must have been a personal question... Wasn't it?

He needed to finish this case and get some distance from Adriana. Because it was getting more and more difficult to keep her at arm's length.

TWELVE

"**A**nything yet?" Adriana asked from where she sat across from Levi at her dining-room table. Levi had asked if they could work on going over case files at her house and she hadn't argued. Especially because he'd promised her Chinese food for dinner.

"Nothing is jumping out at me." He rubbed his head with his hand.

Adriana had been reading an update from her SAR team about what they'd been working on that week, but the look of near defeat on Levi's face made her want to help him. Even if she was eager to get back to the life she was familiar with.

At this point, even if he asked her to step

down, she'd fight him on it. He needed her, whether he wanted to or not.

And she needed to know, strangely, that someone was looking out for him. So far, in all her interactions with him, it had been clear that he was used to being alone. Fending for himself.

Was it wrong to want to be the one who helped him out? Who cared about him?

She had tried over and over again to tamp down those feelings, but so far it hadn't worked. Adriana was close to giving up. To just letting herself care about him, even if he never let her get close. Even if the feelings were never reciprocated.

But what if she got hurt again…?

"I can try looking, if you think it might be worth it," she offered with a shrug.

"I'd appreciate it more than I can say." He exhaled and reached out to hand the papers to her. "Here."

Her fingers brushed his as she took them. Completely accidental, but she was aware of his touch in a curious kind of way.

"Thanks." She cleared her throat, then looked down at the documents. At first she focused on the things she already knew about the victims. Age. General build. It was all what Levi had told her it was.

Goose bumps sprang up on her arms the third time she read over them. Victim number three had been married.

"This woman was cheating on her husband, according to the notes of people who were interviewed. Some friends, but also the man she was cheating with, confirmed it. It's all personal testimony, but it seems pretty for sure."

"Really?" Levi was frowning. "Is nobody faithful these days?"

Adriana shook her head. "That's not it. Some people are. Would be."

That's when he met her eyes, his own eyes widening.

"So... We're looking at a biased cross section of society."

She stopped what she was doing.

"What are you saying?" Adriana asked.

"What if that is one of the things our

victims have in common?" he said aloud, and Adriana felt her own eyes widen as she started shuffling through the pile at double the speed. Levi scooted his chair toward hers and starting looking also.

"Victim number four was also dating a married man."

The same as Raina Marston, though it had only been one date.

How had the killer known? Had they discussed his marriage in the coffee shop? They needed to go back and ask Nathan that.

"Can we link all of them to infidelity of some kind?" Adriana was breathless at the thought that she might have found the link.

"It's looking like it."

Victim one—reports indicated she'd been unfaithful.

Victim two—unknown, but they were curious if more digging would turn up something.

"We need to go back and look at the older murders also."

"If those aren't in the case files, like that kind of information, probably no one knows anymore. Or people would rather not admit to it however many years later."

"Almost thirty years. You have a point."

"Is that what the killer meant, then? As far as rationale?"

Levi stood up and walked across her living room. Then walked back. It was an effortless pace, not frustrated or overly anxious, but it seemed like somehow just the motion of moving helped him to think. And it made Adriana smile because it was just one more part of his personality she thought was fascinating.

"It could be."

His words were hesitant. But his eyes were shining.

They might have finally found a lead. Her heart skipped. She smiled.

Then she yawned as adrenaline finally started to crash and reached up to cover her mouth with a hand. "I'm sorry, this has been fun but tiring."

"Let me order dinner."

She didn't argue with him. He ordered and half an hour later they were eating in relative silence.

"Thanks," Levi said around bites. "For helping with this case, and just being a partner sort of these last few days."

"You don't miss working alone?" she teased him, a smile on her face so he wouldn't misread her tone.

He didn't smile back, though. Instead, he seemed to be thinking. She almost made a joke, anything to lighten the atmosphere that had gotten entirely too serious, but instead she waited, half holding her breath.

"I'm alone too much."

His words were simple, said with a vulnerability that tugged at Adriana's heartstrings. That he could be so honest about something like that attracted her even more, and she found the courage to ask something she hadn't managed to ask before.

"Why haven't you gotten married? I don't believe there hasn't been an opportunity." She didn't need to list his good qualities. Surely he was aware of them.

"I have, actually."

And this was why she had to remember to keep her mouth shut and stay out of other people's business. The quiet hum of the fridge was the only noise, besides the drumming of her fingertips on the tabletop.

She hadn't realized she was drumming. She stilled her hand, shoved it into her lap.

"I am so sorry," she said, shaking her head. She felt her facial muscles tense as she wrestled with regret. Not just for causing awkwardness; she could handle that. What she hated was that she'd hurt Levi. He was one of the people she'd grown to trust and she'd never wanted to cause him pain.

"No, it's okay." He shrugged. "It's just that no one knows, except Judah, of course. I kind of came here to start over."

Something else they had in common, though he didn't know it. Maybe it would be her turn next to share her story.

Rather than being awkward, though, the silence felt full. Adriana took another bite of food. Levi said nothing. They finished eating.

Adriana stood up, took her plate to the sink and was about to ask Levi if he wanted to call it a night and work more in the morning when she heard a noise outside. Sort of a half shuffle, half thump.

Something that sounded very much like someone in her backyard.

"What was that?" she asked, her voice quiet.

Levi's face was unreadable. Completely blank.

"Get in a closet. Somewhere away from the windows. Now."

Fear choked her almost immediately, her throat closing so much that it made swallowing difficult. The events of the last few days, the bodies they'd found, all combined to become an overwhelming force suffocating her body's desire to breathe.

She had to do what Levi said, to push through the panic enough to take shelter.

The pantry was the first place that caught her eye, and she didn't wait for him to tell her twice. She jumped from the table, then flung open the door and fell to the floor. Blue and Babe followed after her. Even with the addition of the dogs, there was room for at least two more people. Not that there were that many of them there who needed to take shelter.

"Levi, aren't you coming in?"

"I need to get whoever this is."

It was like earlier, when he'd insisted she not get in the car and then had started it up on his own. She'd stood there on the deck, farther away from danger, and it had made her feel sick. It felt wrong to let him shoulder all the risk, alone. Even if she was only working with him temporarily, that wasn't what partners did. Not at all.

"No, come in here," she insisted.

"I need to—"

"Levi!" The tone that she used wasn't one she'd heard in ages, probably years. It was every ounce of bossy and "don't take no for an answer" that she possessed, and it worked, because he came to the door and looked at her.

"If you leave, I'm unprotected here. At least, for my sake, stay here." She tried that tactic and saw by the look on his face that he accepted it.

He sat down, pulled the door closed. "Thank you."

She buried her hands in Blue's fur, loving the feel of it between her fingers, fluffy and full.

Levi had pulled out his phone, the light illuminating the mostly dark pantry. The bulb had gone out months ago and she'd never gotten around to replacing it. "Judah, listen, it's Levi. Someone is here, at Adriana's house. Outside. I saw a shadow and Adriana heard a noise. I've got her in an interior closet, the pantry, away from the windows, but I don't like that someone has escalated to stalking."

Was the serial killer escalating, if he'd added stalking to his list of crimes? It was a lesser charge than murder, but it was a different one than those he or she had been committing. Adriana found herself wondering, mostly to keep her mind occupied.

"Thanks," Levi said and disconnected, rubbing the back of his neck. "Someone will be right over." He looked at the door again, like he was considering leaving.

"Please," she said again. He nodded. She reached for his hand, truly more for reassurance than anything. She only meant to squeeze it once. But he tightened his grip.

And didn't let go.

His phone screen went black. They were back in the dark.

Then there was silence again. Levi broke it, in a voice barely above a whisper.

"I was married once."

He felt closer in the darkness. The conversation felt more natural.

"What...?" Her voice trailed off, curiosity making her ask the question and then self-consciousness making her immediately wonder if she should have. She wanted to know. But she didn't want him to feel like he had to tell her.

She could still barely breathe, though the pressure on her chest had eased slightly. Listening to his voice seemed to do that, make her calm down.

"She divorced me, five years ago. After she cheated on me. Then died a couple of years later. Car accident."

To have had a loss doubled like that… Adriana couldn't even imagine that, so didn't say anything.

"I guess you probably… I mean, I guess it answers your question. I did try the marriage thing. I wasn't very good at it. So. Now you know."

Adriana could barely breathe. Her chest was tight with his pain, with knowing that he blamed himself. Adriana wasn't stupid. She knew that every relationship took two people and when a relationship broke up both usually had roles to play.

But she'd also seen friends' marriages end without their permission, despite everything they'd desperately tried to patch up that someone else had willingly broken.

"It wasn't your fault." He'd said the

woman had cheated on him. Couldn't he see that took the blame away from him for their broken relationship? Did he see that he could have a second chance, start over?

Her heart pounded in her chest, suddenly aware of his proximity in a way that related to more than just safety.

"I wasn't good at marriage. I guess some people just aren't meant for relationships." All she knew was that rather than say all that she was thinking, Adriana leaned toward him. Then she caught herself. Was she really doing this?

She could see the silhouette of his face in the dark, close to her, but not close enough. He moved another inch or two toward her.

She reached up, brushed his cheek with her hand, feeling the stubble along it. Definitely not just a friendly gesture.

There was no going back now. Adriana lifted her face to his and met his lips with hers. It was a kiss unlike any she'd had before. A whisper of reassurance in the dark, something not slow and lingering, but not fast and passionate, either. It was firm. Steady. Soft.

The man might say he wasn't good at relationships, but man, could he kiss. Adriana kissed him back, leaning closer to him as she did so.

For the first time since she could remember, she felt like she wasn't alone.

She felt safe.

Levi didn't know how they'd gone from talking about what a failure he was to kissing, but then her lips were on his and he couldn't have argued with that if he'd tried.

He did know when to pull away, though, and did so, although he felt breathless. When she'd kissed him, he'd forgotten his questions about whether there was something wrong with him that made him too broken for relationships. No, when she kissed him, nothing in him felt broken. She was like healing and wholeness, or at least the reminder of the fact that those could be possible, wrapped up in one beautiful package… One who was kissing him. Alone. In a dark closet. That was why he'd needed to pull away.

Because he wanted to do this right. He wanted to be good at relationships, starting with making sure he didn't promise something more than he was willing to give right now.

Besides all that, she might still be in danger. He needed every sense on alert right now for what might be happening outside.

When she was kissing him? She was all any of his senses noticed.

She was certainly a distraction.

He swallowed hard.

"I'm not sorry," she said, head still close to his. Their foreheads were almost touching and he could feel her breath on his cheek. "Please, please don't say you're sorry. Are you?"

He wouldn't, because he wasn't. But, oh, what had he been thinking? They'd been working together so well, and everything could be jeopardized because of that kiss.

But everything was possible because of that kiss, too. The second chance he'd never really thought he could have was sitting in front of him in a darkened pantry.

His phone beeped.

"My brother's here." Levi stood, and Adriana did, too. They were still close together. And somehow it didn't make Levi want to back away. Instead, he fought the desire to pull her toward him and kiss her again.

"Are you okay?" she asked, softly, like the walls between them were gone. Like she cared and wasn't afraid to show it and wasn't afraid who knew.

"Adriana?" He turned to her, intending to speak, but her full lips caught his eye, and he closed his eyes to kiss her one more time. Softly, with purpose.

"Yes?" she answered after breaking off the contact, sounding as stunned by the entire situation as he felt.

"That question you asked earlier? I'm not sorry, either," he said and stepped out into the light of the kitchen, heading toward the front door.

His heart was still pounding when he got to the front door, and not from the danger, either. This time it was something else entirely.

Some*one* else.

How many years had he known Adriana and just been driven crazy by things about her that now made him feel captivated? Timing was a funny thing.

Maybe he hadn't been ready before.

Was he now? He shook off the question before it could fully land, the feeling of her lips on his still fresh in his mind. The way it felt to have someone look at him like he mattered, like they trusted him.

He wanted to be the type of man she clearly thought he was.

Someone knocked on the door. He took his hand off his sidearm, where he'd placed it just in case, moved the blinds up from the door to confirm that it was Judah, then unlocked the door and let him in. "Thanks for coming," he said. "Nothing out there?"

Judah shook his head as he stepped inside. Levi locked the door behind him. "No *one* out there, anyway. I wouldn't say there was nothing."

"What does that mean?"

Judah handed a note to him. Levi frowned. Whoever was after them had already shot at them and blown up his car. A note made no sense if the killer had appeared to be escalating.

Stop working the case. They deserved their judgment. It was necessary punishment. You and your girlfriend have done nothing wrong, but you have made yourself a target if you won't leave this case alone.

Levi blinked. The words were typed. So writing it must have been premeditated. It was essentially the same message of the phone call, but with more urgency.

The serial killer felt justified for what he

or she had been doing. It didn't surprise Levi too much. It was a special kind of insanity, but this was consistent with it.

It made the person that much more dangerous, though, because they had a level of determination that someone committing a general crime of passion might not have.

"So whoever is behind this sent me a warning. And Adriana, too."

Judah nodded.

He could handle the threat against himself. It certainly wasn't the first time. But the idea that Adriana's life was in danger grated at him, and would have even if they hadn't kissed earlier.

What had made the killer assume she was his girlfriend? Was it a sarcastic comment? Or had someone seen them together so much they'd truly assumed that?

Either way, she was in danger, which Levi hated.

She had done nothing to deserve that kind of threat. She wasn't even officially after the killer. *He* was.

Maybe Judah had been right. He should never have let her get involved.

All the places he'd taken her, the danger he put her in over and over, went through his mind. From the darkened woods where they searched for bodies, to the fact that he'd taken her with him to the coffee shop and to talk to Nathan Hall, frustration boiled over. He couldn't believe himself.

What had he been thinking?

He needed to talk to Nathan Hall again. If they were being warned off the case *now*, there had to be a reason. Something about their investigation today had triggered the serial killer's rage.

Which meant that they were getting close. But he wasn't taking her with him this time, not when it could put her in more danger.

"I've got to go somewhere." Levi glanced over his shoulder, in the direction of Adriana. "Can you stay here with her for me?"

Judah nodded. "No problem. You'll be careful?"

"Yes."

Levi gathered his things and headed for the front door. Outside, there was a replacement patrol car that one of the officers had brought by earlier.

He stopped one more time before walking out.

"Watch out for her." Levi met his brother's eyes, which were overflowing with questions. Yeah, well, he'd answer them later. Or maybe not. Right now he needed to know she'd be okay long enough for him to have the conversation with her that he needed to have.

"I will." Judah nodded.

And God, if You're listening, please take care of her, too. He added the prayer as he reached for the door, trying in one tiny step to trust the God he had walked away from.

"What's going on?" Adriana walked into her entryway just in time to see Levi reaching for the door. He was leaving? Without saying goodbye?

"I've got to go talk to Nathan Hall

again." He hesitated, then walked toward her. "My brother is staying here with you. Be safe and don't go outside, okay?" He pulled her toward him, like it was something he'd done a hundred times, and kissed the top of her forehead. It felt familiar. Like he'd done it a hundred times before. Safe. Warm.

Loving? "I'll be back soon."

Judah locked the door behind Levi and looked back at Adriana.

Her cheeks heated under his gaze and she heard his unasked questions.

"Please be careful. I don't want to see him get hurt," Judah finally said, bypassing anything resembling a question and going straight for his point.

She fought the urge to be offended, which was balanced by her appreciation of how much Judah cared about his brother.

She nodded. "Okay."

Judah considered her again. "He's been hurt before."

"He told me," she said, wanting him to know that she wasn't being casual about this. And from the way he'd pulled her close, it didn't feel like it was casual to Levi, either.

"He's never going to stop being a police officer," Judah said.

Why would he? Adriana had had the privilege to watch him this week, and he was good at his job. She'd never ask him to do that.

She frowned. "Right, I know."

"Good." Judah nodded once, like that was all he needed to hear. "I've got some work to do on my computer. If you don't mind, I'd rather stay inside where I'm closer to you."

She would prefer that also. Adriana nodded. "Thank you."

True to his word, Judah walked away to the living room. Adriana went toward the kitchen. Strange that he'd brought up Levi being a police officer. Was that related to what had gone wrong in his marriage? She didn't feel like it was her place to ask necessarily...

But she meant what she'd said to Judah.

She would never ask Levi to give that up, even if they started some kind of relationship.

She reached for a dish in the sink and started to scrub. Levi was at this minute at the house of a man who could be a murderer. Maybe he wasn't. But he could be.

Okay, if she thought really hard about it she could understand why a woman who cared about a man wouldn't love him being in constant danger. She and Levi, though…they weren't anything yet.

Adriana just needed to know if she could live with that.

She reached for another dish, scrubbed harder and tried not to think.

THIRTEEN

"You didn't tell me everything earlier," Levi said once a surprised Nathan Hall had opened the door and invited him inside.

The other man looked like a weasel, his eyes wide, his nose practically twitching with nerves. Levi supposed that was what happened when you were trying to live a double life and half of it kept trying to catch you out.

"I didn't," he admitted.

Good. Levi liked it when people didn't bother to argue with him or lie to him. It made his job much easier that way.

"We talked about why you were out dating, and then we left to investigate another lead. I didn't ask you how you and Raina parted, and as it turns out, that is very important also."

"Like, was she mad? Or...?"

"No." Levi shook his head. "Did you walk her to her car at the coffee shop? Did you drive her to your place? Her place? Where did you go after coffee? And where did she go?"

Now he wanted to lead the man, as it was all too easy to guess that he'd gone back to one of their houses and they'd done things he didn't want to admit to.

"Nothing happened" was all Nathan said.

Levi stared. Kept staring.

The guy finally broke after a few tense seconds. "We were supposed to go back to her place, okay? But you can go there and search it, however you guys do, and you'll know I was never there. I waited in the driveway for a solid half hour, and she never showed. Do you know how embarrassing that is? It's not like it was even my home, where I could go about my business—I'm just sitting in some woman's driveway and she's who knows where."

"Getting murdered, probably, in this case." Levi didn't sugarcoat it.

Nathan paled.

"I need you to tell me every detail you remember about your conversation."

He nodded, then swallowed hard. "Okay, I can do that."

Forty minutes later, Levi left again. According to Nathan, he and Raina had hit it off at the coffee shop. They'd started talking and he'd thought things were going well. That's when they'd made the plan to meet back at her house. They'd left at the same time. She never showed up.

If he was telling the truth, something Levi generally had a fairly good sense about, then she had been abducted somewhere between the coffee shop and her house.

There had been no cell phone on her person when they'd recovered her body. If there was, they could have used the GPS to track her movements. As it was, that wasn't an option. So he had to think through others.

The presence of more traffic cameras in town would have made everything easier as another option. But Raven Pass didn't have many. Without the cell phone tracker or cameras to work with, they would need to talk to anyone who was in the area at the time.

How had someone known to come after Raina, though? It was another hole in the case he needed to figure out. Had someone recognized one of them and then decided to enact what they saw as justice? Or had someone heard them talking in the coffee shop and then decided to kill her?

He thought about the barista's binder. Was there a chance they could find someone that way, through the receipts? Only if they'd paid by credit card. It was a possibility, but not a good one.

It might be a better decision to work the case from another angle.

Levi drove back to Adriana's house, the thought of facing her again making butterflies dance in his stomach. Since they'd kissed, he'd been focused on this discussion with Nathan.

Now he had a chance to think about what they'd done.

And he still wasn't sorry.

He parked the patrol car in the driveway, beside his brother's, and knocked on the door. Judah answered it, and Levi walked inside.

"Everything okay?"

"It's been quiet. Nothing going on."

Levi looked at his brother and tried to gauge what else he wasn't saying. He wouldn't have talked to Adriana about that kiss Levi had given her as he left, would he?

Thinking back on it, though, yes, he might have. Because Levi hadn't just hugged her like a casual friend. He'd pulled her to him and kissed her head like she was his to embrace and say goodbye to and expect she'd be waiting for him. It had been the gesture of someone who was part of a couple. Not friends. Not co-workers.

"Did you say something to her?" he asked, his suspicions high.

"I just don't want you hurt."

Well, that answered that question.

Levi shook his head. "Don't mess with my personal life, okay? I don't need your interfering." Would he always feel like the little brother? He had no problem being younger, not in theory. He'd be in good shape longer and would be able to work longer, both of which were perks. But he was tired of being the one looked down on as less experienced.

It was partially his fault for not making wise choices earlier in life. But he was doing better now.

"Never meant to interfere." Serious as usual, Judah shook his head and started toward the door. "I figured it was you at the door, so I got my things together. Officer Koser is watching her house tonight, so let me know when you're planning to leave and I'll send him over."

Or maybe Levi should call Koser himself, so his brother didn't know exactly what time he left and question him about that. Wisely, he kept those thoughts to himself and just nodded.

He didn't want to antagonize Judah. He just needed him to treat him like the adult he was.

"Have a good night." Levi offered a small olive branch.

"You, too," Judah said, and then he left. Levi locked the door behind him.

Levi walked into the living room, expecting to see Adriana, but she wasn't there. He frowned and walked toward the kitchen.

She was scrubbing at the top of the oven, which looked perfectly clean to him.

"Everything okay?" he asked quietly so he didn't scare her.

She still jumped and he didn't blame her. It had been a tense few days. "Levi, you startled me."

"You're all right?" Was she upset about the kiss? The danger they were in?

About nothing at all?

It had been so long since he wondered

what a woman was thinking, he'd forgotten exactly how relationships worked. Did he push her to tell him or let it go?

See, he really wasn't very good at this. A good reason if there ever was one to apologize to Adriana for the kiss and gracefully bow out of whatever it was he had started.

But if he did that, he'd lose her. And that wasn't a good option, either.

Levi took a deep breath and waited. Better let her answer before he stressed too much.

"I'm okay," she sighed, then shrugged. "I was just worried."

He stepped toward her. "Judah was here. You were totally fine."

She looked up at him and he stepped closer. They were close enough to touch, but they didn't—but he still felt her closeness as much as if they were.

"I wasn't worried about me, I was worried about… You know what, it doesn't matter." She smiled. "Never mind."

"You're okay now?" he asked.

She smiled and nodded. "I'm okay."

He reached out, rubbed her shoulder, and she moved closer toward him.

"Levi?"

Her eyes asked him questions that her lips never asked. What were they doing? Was this the start of something or just a weird reaction to the pressure they were under and all the time they'd been spending together?

He didn't have answers to any of it, not tonight, so instead of trying, he just hugged her close to him, loving how much smaller than him she was. She melted into his embrace and he felt his shoulders relax, even as his mind grew firmer in its resolve.

He had to protect this woman he was slowly coming to love.

Had to.

"It's all going to be okay," he told her, hoping that he was telling her the truth.

Usually at night, Adriana was asleep moments after her head hit the pillow, but tonight she heard every creak of the house, every car door slamming from down her street, every strange dream-inspired noise that Blue made.

Levi had *kissed* her.

And then walked into the house of someone they weren't sure was innocent of murder. He'd faced down a possible killer, giving little to no thought for his own safety.

She had meant what she said to Judah, that she could never imagine asking Levi to give up his job. But she hadn't expected to spend the next hour after that unable to concentrate on anything as worries for Levi clamored for her attention in her head.

Could she let herself fall for a cop? She'd already lost one man she'd loved. And Robert had had a desk job, working for the Alaska Department of Fish and Game. But his hobbies had been full of risks, and ultimately one had been responsible for the loss of his life. Should she let herself fall for someone who put himself at more risk than that on a regular basis? Knowing the danger he would be in every day he went to work and even on his days off?

The darkness held no answers and she turned over again. Blue cuddled closer against her. She'd once had a no-dogs-on-the-bed policy, but Blue had broken her of that. Babe preferred to sleep on the floor, have his own space.

What do I do, God? Do I keep moving forward with whatever this is? He hadn't kissed her good-night, but the way he'd held her still made her feel the closeness between them. Everything was different now. Funny how one small kiss could break down so many walls.

They'd decided to spend the next day with Blue, checking out the four sites where they knew the killer had buried bodies, in case there had been additional victims. It could be a pattern.

The more evidence they found, the better their chances of catching the killer got. If Adriana and Blue could find what Levi thought they would tomorrow, they'd have enough for him to finish building his case without her and her dog's help. It might be the last day they would need to work together.

Was it because he was developing feelings for her that he was pulling away with the case? Was he trying to keep her safe and out of it?

It had to be that, because nothing about the way he'd behaved tonight implied that he wanted to see her less. If anything, it was the opposite.

She turned over again. Men were confusing. She needed to fall asleep so she could wake up for work. At least her job made sense.

FOURTEEN

The drive to the site of the first body was much like it had been days before.

"You ready for today?" Levi asked her, and Adriana nodded and petted her dog.

"I hope so." She patted Blue, trying not to let her nerves show in her voice. They were going to see whether they could find three, or even all four, bodies in one day.

It would be a lot for Blue, and for her, but she had dog treats and toys for the dog; she'd ordered herself a new ebook to read in the bubble bath she was planning to take tonight.

They parked the car and climbed out, then headed to the trailhead. Waiting for them there were Wren and Judah.

"I asked Wren to meet us up here today,

in case we were successful," Levi explained after hugging his cousin and nodding good-morning to his brother.

Adriana said hello, too, and found herself wishing she could have been alone with Levi on what would likely be the last day before he went back to work on his own.

They were both busy, driven people. Wasn't that a recipe for drifting apart?

They'd stalled out before they began.

Maybe.

She and Levi had discussed the way she worked and decided that today it was better for Blue to be on a leash. Her dog could otherwise catch a scent of another body, if any others were buried out here; they wanted to focus on the specific area they were suspicious about, not just shoot blindly.

The pressure of the dog pulling on the leash was comforting and familiar to her this morning. With so many other aspects of her life feeling like question marks, the relationship with her dog was a constant.

"It's about half a mile up ahead," Levi said.
"That's it?"

He nodded. They walked in silence.
Judah and Wren were behind them, but
they weren't talking much, either. Adriana caught them looking at Blue once or
twice, which was a good thing. Judah had
always been one of those officers who
didn't put a lot of stock in what her dog
said. It would be good for him to watch
them work.

Adriana had given Blue the scent at
the parking lot, and she knew what she
was looking for. Levi had asked how that
worked, for a cadaver dog, and Adriana
had explained that they sometimes used
artificial scents when training the animals. Blue was trained to alert to both
deceased bodies and live missing persons
whose scents she'd been tracking, so when
they were searching for cadavers, Adriana
liked to give her that synthetic scent to
remind her which they were looking for.
Adriana watched her take in the area, with

her nose, her eyes, her ears. All senses were engaged.

Blue's demeanor changed. She perked her ears and held herself more upright, even as her face somehow got sadder. The facial expression was not a standard search-dog alert technique, but Adriana felt she knew her dog.

"She's got it," Adriana said and checked her GPS watch. They'd gone just about half a mile.

Right where they'd wandered about last time. She stole a glance at Levi. His expression was intent, determination in his eyes.

They were so close.

"Good girl, keep going," Adriana said as Blue nosed the ground, still moving forward. They followed her, cutting through the low vegetation. Adriana tried to step as carefully as possible. There was no sign of anyone walking this way recently, but then again the bodies they were looking for were from several decades ago. The ground would have healed.

The families who didn't have closure would not have.

Blue whined, low and long, and dropped to her stomach.

Bingo.

Adriana nodded. Levi stopped and they waited for Wren and Judah to catch up.

"That's it?" Wren asked.

"Yes," Adriana confirmed.

Wren walked toward the site, paced around where Blue was lying down, looking like she was studying the ground itself.

Wren cleared the ground as best she could and studied it again. Then she started to dig.

Adriana stood and watched as long as she could, though heaviness pressed against her as she thought of what they were doing, of what had been done and how evil people could be. She just wasn't cut out for this kind of work, and it had never been more apparent to her.

Many of her acquaintances who were in law enforcement all seemed to handle it better than she did. But Ellie had confided in her once that she'd been in law enforcement before coming to Alaska. She hadn't offered any more details than that, and Adriana hadn't asked for them.

It was part of the bond of the far north, in a way. People who came here had reasons, some of which people didn't want to talk about. But you understood, even if none of you spoke of them.

"You okay?" Levi asked. Had he really learned to read her that well over just a few days?

Adriana shook her head. "I'm going to walk a bit."

Levi nodded. "Let me come with you."

"No, I'm okay."

Judah approached. "I'll go, then."

Levi looked at his brother.

"I know you want to see what Wren finds," Judah reasoned. "And I also know Adriana doesn't need to be alone. Especially not here."

Adriana didn't argue, just started walking across the open alpine landscape.

Whichever brother followed her was fine with her because she didn't necessarily want to be alone right now, anyway. Not so close to where a killer had already buried one victim.

What if he was watching? He already seemed to know so much about where they were, what they were doing.

Were they being followed?

She shook her head and took a deep breath of fresh air, trying to clear her mind of all the clutter from the case.

"I'm behind you, just so you don't get startled," Judah called.

"Thanks." She didn't mind that Levi hadn't come. She didn't want to talk right now, anyway.

No, right now she wanted to think about the world they lived in, where some person would end someone else's life. Where hikers got lost and were found dead, with hands zip-tied.

Where her fiancé could be out for a fun snowmobile ride and never return.

Why did God let it all happen? It wasn't

like this was the first time she'd asked—
she'd asked many times over the years—
but the need for answers pressed heavy
on her now, with this case added to her
questions.

It was time for her to decide what she
believed still, about God. For years she'd
wrestled with the discomfort of knowing
God had allowed tragedy into her life.
With a deep personal knowledge that God
allowed bad things to happen.

She felt more than ever like this case
was drawing her toward a decision point.
Did she still trust Him, or not?

And still, that resounding question she
had. Unanswered. *Why?*

Why? Why? Why?

God didn't answer, through either a
small voice or any kind of booming thun-
der. Instead, there was just wind across
the mountainside tundra. A marmot calling somewhere.

A beautiful, gorgeous world God had
created.

Adriana stopped trying to wrestle with

these big questions. Right now she bent down and scratched her dog behind the ears.

"You doing okay, sweetie?" she asked her.

Blue looked up, big brown eyes kind. Concerned.

"Yeah, I'm okay if you are," Adriana whispered. "It's just not my favorite way to spend a day. But three more and we are done."

She walked back toward the site of the body and found that they'd unearthed a large object wrapped in trash bags. Exactly the right size to be a body. Adriana looked away.

"Judah, if you'll stay here while Wren finishes up, Adriana and I will move on."

"You're going to look at the three other places?"

Levi nodded.

This was the body closest to Raven Pass. There was one more a bit farther away, then one closer to Girdwood, which was only about a fifteen-minute drive, maybe twenty. The farthest away was near the town of Hope.

That meant they'd have to spend the entire day together, in order to make all those drives.

And surely they wouldn't excavate each body? It was fall and so the sunshine was no longer endless. Days had their nights now, natural stopping points for work. "We won't be able to unbury all of them today, right?" she asked, hoping the answer was no. This had felt enough like an eerie backward burial to her, and she couldn't handle the weight of any more of them today.

"No. We'll mark them with GPS coordinates so I can come back when you aren't with us."

Apparently he'd read all her struggles on her face. And while Adriana didn't like feeling like the weak link, it was okay. She nodded. "Thanks."

They hiked back in silence and wasted no time getting to the second location.

Blue found the next body within an hour of starting their hike, though this time it had taken her a little longer to pinpoint the exact location. It was about fifteen feet, Levi had said aloud earlier, from where they'd found a body during this most recent investigation. The last one had been twenty feet away, so it appeared the exact distance between the two bodies wasn't part of an MO, but the fact that there were two indicated a pattern.

She'd learned more fascinating facts about serial killers, their inconsistencies and idiosyncrasies, during the last week than she'd ever wanted to know.

"Want to go to Hope or Girdwood first?"

North or south. May as well get the easy one out of the way so they could devote the rest of the day to the one that would be more of a challenge.

"Girdwood, then Hope," she suggested.

He nodded his agreement, and they climbed back in the car with Blue and started the drive.

They had quick success with the body just off the popular Winner Creek Trail in Girdwood. He remembered being there when this crime scene had been worked a few years ago, for the body they'd found then. They'd been on high alert as it had been berry season at the time and grizzly bears were thick in these woods. Now it was late enough in the year that bears should be thinking about bedding down, but he still didn't let his guard down, not until they'd entered the GPS coordinates and made it back to the car.

Only the body in Hope was left. As far as Levi could tell, Blue was doing better today. Her general body language still seemed good and she was wagging her tail, chewing the caribou antler Adriana had given her for a treat after they'd loaded back up in the car.

She'd told him in one of their earlier conversations that while working animals were usually given a treat after making their find, many cadaver dogs wouldn't take the treat in the presence of a body. They could tell just by the smell that something was wrong, and it made them feel disconcerted. Off.

Adriana seemed to feel the same as the dog. She was the main reason he was in a hurry to get this done. While he'd enjoyed the time spent with her, he'd watched her over the last few days and this case was adding shadows underneath her eyes that he didn't like to see there. Not because they hurt her beauty at all—they didn't. She was gorgeous no matter what. But because they were a reflection of how she felt inside and he didn't want that tiredness or hopelessness for her.

"Are you going to be okay for one more?" he asked as he turned left onto the Seward Highway from Girdwood. This road would take them back past the turnoff for Raven Pass and then onward to the Kenai Peninsula and Hope. He'd only been to the town of Hope once, years ago one July, when Jim had talked him into going fishing there. He'd had some fun, but the fishing was better down near Soldotna, at least in Levi's opinion. The longer drive was worth it to him.

"I can handle one more." She said the words like she was hoping she believed them.

"Thank you for doing this."

"Well, we need to finish." She allowed a small smile.

"I meant all of it. You didn't have to help at all, but frankly I'd have been lost without you. And not just because if I'd had to find that first burial site near the lake without you, I'd probably still be looking. Nothing I know of substitutes for a search dog in cases like that. I owe you, really."

She shook her head. "You don't. I wanted to help."

The air between them was thick and Levi wasn't sure what had happened between last night and now, at least between them.

Eighteen or so hours ago they'd been kissing in her pantry, hardly any space between them. Now she was quiet, her answers short.

And he was no expert at relationships, but it still felt to him like something was wrong.

"While we're driving," he began, keeping his eyes on the road, "we should talk."

"About?"

"We kissed last night." Remarkably, he got the words out without tripping over them, though when he thought back to that kiss, his mind felt like a muddle of all good things and it was hard to focus. It was a wonder he'd been able to talk even semi-articulately about it.

"We did." She matched his tone with her own unflinching one, which he appreciated. That was one of the things he loved about Adriana, her confidence.

He…what?

Levi swallowed hard. "We, uh…" And now any focus he'd had was gone. Love? *Love?* Sure, he'd been planning this conversation, hoping to ask her to date, but now…

The calm he'd felt was gone, evaporated like morning dew. In its place was a feeling of being tossed about, akin to the waves he was watching in Turnagain Arm right now as they drove down the highway. The water was a churning steely gray.

That was what his mind felt like when it thought for too long about the word *love*. Love hadn't been good to him, not so far. Friends, he could do. Kissing he could do, at least with Adriana. They'd proved that.

But he'd wanted to date her. To what purpose?

Did he not remember he'd tried this relationship road before and failed?

"Was there something you wanted to talk to me about, Levi?"

Suddenly, something slammed into the back of him, sending his car jerking toward the center line.

Adriana screamed and grabbed her dog, who had slammed into Levi's shoulder in the initial impact.

"Hang on!" Levi corrected himself toward the right, got them back in their lane quickly enough to avoid the large moving van that had been coming toward them in the other lane.

"What was that?" Her voice trembled, betraying her fear in its unsteadiness, and Levi had nothing with which to reassure her.

This serial killer usually killed his victims up close, forensic evidence said. But Levi had felt relatively calm when he'd been shot at because from the beginning, it had somehow felt like a warning to him. Then the bomb had happened and it had confirmed his suspicions.

Their lives had only been in a semblance of danger.

Now, the real thing began. Because the killer was almost within arm's reach. And for the many victims who had come before, that point was exactly when they'd died.

Levi wasn't going to let that happen, not to Adriana. At least not without a fight.

He glanced over at her.

He wouldn't let anything happen to her dog, either. She'd never forgive him if he did. And she didn't deserve to lose anyone else she cared about.

The car slammed into him again.

Levi jerked the wheel left, into a parking lot near Portage, trying to lose the car, but it followed. He floored it back onto the highway.

"What are you doing?" Adriana's voice, coming from between clenched teeth, demanded an answer.

"Trying to keep us alive."

"And you think getting involved in some kind of high-speed chase is the best way to accomplish that?" she asked, her eyes on the side-view mirror. He knew that because he'd looked over at her before.

The car was getting closer.

There was little other traffic today, but he was still worried there would be some kind of casualties if he didn't get off the road soon.

Clearly their would-be killer wasn't giving up easily.

"Get your phone out and call 911," he told her, trying to keep his voice as calm as he could.

Adriana did what he asked, and he was proud of her for the way she relayed the information like the trained professional she was.

That was the thing about her he didn't think she realized. She might not like the darkness. But she sure could withstand it better than almost anyone he'd ever met. She buckled down, found some kind of strength inside, maybe from God, and made it through.

Yeah, no matter how scared it made him, he loved her.

And he might have missed the chance to tell her. You didn't get a second chance to say some things.

He hoped he got a second chance for that conversation that he'd handled badly.

Because if he lived, he was going to ask Adriana if she'd be willing to date a guy who wasn't very good at relationships, since there was a very good possibility that guy was head over heels for her.

FIFTEEN

Adriana watched the speedometer creep
over eighty, so she gripped the door handle of the car tighter. Eighty might not be
fast on some roads, but on the notoriously
dangerous Seward Highway, with sheer
cliffs on one side and ocean on the other,
it was terrifying.

"We've got to figure something out,"
Adriana said as they advanced on a Win-
nebago camper and Levi passed it, cutting
it close. The SUV chasing them followed
and advanced on them again.

They were going to be hit again, while
going… She glanced at the dashboard
again.

Ninety miles per hour wouldn't go well.
This wasn't working. It was too much of

a risk, and besides, staying on the road would endanger the other drivers.

Did they have other options? she asked herself as she dug her fingers into Blue's fur, trying not to grip too tightly, and fought to maintain some semblance of composure.

They could pull over, but with as few cars as were on the road today, there wouldn't be many witnesses. They could be killed in plain sight and still it was possible that no one might see.

They could keep going, but it might cause a wreck, hurting innocent people, one that she and Levi couldn't survive.

"We could go back to Raven Pass?" she offered, but it was still another few miles up the road.

"That's my plan."

Adriana kept looking in the side-view mirror. Then she looked up at the road. One or two more miles to Raven Pass.

Levi eased off the gas. Put his right turn signal on.

And made the turn off the main highway.

The SUV kept going straight.

His hands free, Levi called the police department and reported the incident.

Adriana's heart raced in her chest, maybe worse now. She was usually okay during an immediate crisis that required her focus, she'd learned.

Now, though, now that there was a break in the danger, she felt like she was going to be sick.

"I never should have let you do this." Levi's voice was emotionless. Numb.

Yet somehow, the words still cut her to the quick. "You just told me you couldn't have done it without me." Something warned her not to talk, to be patient, to be kind. But she ignored that. How could he have said that less than half an hour earlier and now be claiming he never should have let her help?

It made no sense and it was insulting. Not to mention pointless. Clearly they couldn't change the past. So why waste time saying things that would only hurt people's feelings?

"I... Maybe I couldn't have. I know it would have taken ages longer, but I had no right to ask you to risk your safety."

"You didn't ask, I offered," she reminded him, feeling her patience wearing thin. She heard it in her voice, the harsh edges of frustration. It wasn't anger with him, she reminded herself. It had been a traumatic experience just now. A traumatic week, really.

"But I—"

"You know, Levi, you can't make other people's decisions for them. You can't decide that I shouldn't have helped you. You can't decide anything except what has to do with you. You can't decide that because you were married once and it ended badly that you're never going to let anyone else love you." The last part came out in one big whoosh of breath.

Adriana gasped as she realized what she'd said. Had she consciously known she loved him until she said that? No, but she did. It was true.

But it didn't need to be said now, not in

a long tirade like that when she'd thrown his past in his face, even if it was meant to be an encouragement that he could one day have a better future. And it wasn't like she'd even had the courage to say she loved him, to tell him he could have a future *now*.

She'd just tossed out his past failure and berated him with it.

"I'm sorry. I'm so sorry," she said quickly, but not quickly enough.

Pain had etched itself across Levi's face.

Subtlety had never been her strong point, but she didn't generally go for the jugular in conversations. She'd hurt him just now, mentioning how his marriage had ended badly. She'd unintentionally used that as a weapon. She hadn't meant to, but that didn't mean it was less painful. And there was nothing she could do to undo that.

"Levi…" She trailed off. All her apologies would go unacknowledged.

He nodded. "Yeah, you're right."

She stilled. "Oh, yeah?"

He turned down one street, then another. Then onto hers.

He parked in her driveway and met her eyes. "I can't decide not to let anyone love me, but I can sure decide not to love anyone else."

She felt the words stab her heart like a knife. Like hers must have felt to him earlier. She nodded. Swallowed hard. "Thanks for driving me home."

She had so many questions that weren't going to be answered. Why had the SUV tried to run them off the road and then backed off? When Levi ran the plates, who would the car come up as registered to?

He was the officer. He would learn the answers to those questions and have no reason to tell her. Because even though it hadn't been said, Adriana knew she was done with this investigation. Levi would leave the last burial site alone, or go without her.

They were finished, too.

Whatever of "them" there had been. It

was just a kiss or two. Nothing that should have rocked her world the way it did, but maybe it was for the best. She didn't know why right now, but the empty platitude was all she had to offer herself.

A verse about God working for good to those who were "called according to his purpose" came to her mind. She didn't remember where it was from, but welcomed the reminder that God works things out for His people.

Maybe things would work out. Or maybe this *was* them working out.

"Goodbye, Levi."

He nodded to her. "I'll stay until someone else gets here."

Adriana nodded. She'd long since stopped fighting the extra security. She wanted to *live*.

And she wanted to fall in love again. Even if that meant risks.

She'd wanted to let herself fall in love with Levi. Actually, she already had. It just looked like she was the only one who'd let her mind go there.

"Thanks." She opened the car door and exited with Blue. "For everything," she said with finality, and then walked inside.

Once the door was all the way shut, she finally let herself cry. For Levi, for Robert, for all of it.

Idiot. Idiot. Idiot. Levi didn't know what he was upset with himself for most. Starting that conversation in the car? Abandoning it when he'd panicked? Or planning to tell Adriana that he loved her and then blowing up any chance they'd had at a relationship after she'd made a careless comment that had hurt him?

Calling it careless wasn't exactly true. He was pretty sure she'd meant it to hurt him, at least in some way, but they'd just had a near-death experience. She'd been tense, angry, boiling over with frustration.

Instead of answering in a kind voice and calming down, he'd reacted, too. And now it was too late to fix anything. He'd seen the shuttered look come over her eyes.

He wasn't the only one who had been

hurt in the past. And now they'd both hurt each other again.

See, this was why he should focus on his work and not people. Because people did let you down, even when they loved you.

He had no idea how some people made it work. Like his parents, who had been married for thirty-five years. Or Jim, who'd been married for somewhere around forty at this point. His thirty-fifth anniversary had been when he'd still worked at the police department. They'd had a cake for him.

He should call her and apologize, and see if there was any way they could…

What? There was nothing to do. Nothing to patch up.

Did he call and try to mend their friendship at least?

Judah was at her house now. He'd tried to get another officer to do it, but had finally had to accept that he was the only one with the time.

"Just leave her alone about me, okay?

There's nothing going on anymore," he'd said to his brother.

Judah had just raised his eyebrows. "I'm not your dating coach."

Sure, *now* he wanted to be uninvolved.

Levi had gone to the police department to meet with Wren, who had information on the bodies they'd recovered today. She'd called in some colleagues to help with the sheer volume of work, but all three victims were from over two decades ago. Female.

More details would emerge with time, but so far they fit the profile.

One victim from the first set of murders. One victim from the most recent set. None in between. When Adriana had the idea to help, Levi had been so sure he'd find a link between both cases, and that the link would be in the form of murder committed between then and now.

Instead there were no bodies from that time frame.

The killer had truly stopped killing for over twenty years.

Levi paced his office, then sat down in his chair. He'd promised himself he wouldn't bother Jim and would let the man enjoy his retirement, but there was one question he wanted someone else's perspective on.

And now he couldn't get Adriana's.

He picked up the phone, dialed and listened to it ring.

"Levi, how are you doing? How's the case?" Jim's voice was warm, as usual, with a smile.

"I'm good. A little stuck, actually, on the case, so I wanted to get your thoughts on something."

"Please do. I'm stuck at home watching romance movies." He lowered his voice. "And if I have to watch another one I'm going to lose my mind."

Levi suppressed a laugh. He supposed that was one small bright side of how badly things had ended between him and Adriana before they even began.

Then an image of her, tucked into a fleece blanket, on his couch watching a predictable Christmas movie crossed his mind.

It almost made it hard to breathe; that was how much he wanted the future he envisioned. How much he wanted her in his life.

He'd go back over tonight and talk to her. Maybe she wouldn't forgive him right away, but surely he could have one more chance, right?

Adriana was special, different. The only second chance he wanted in his life. He didn't want to lose her.

Jim cleared his throat. "You okay?"

Levi hadn't been paying attention, and as usual his old partner had noticed. The man seemed to notice everything.

"Yeah, uh, I'm fine. Listen, Jim. I meant to leave you out of this case and let you just enjoy being retired."

"Like I said. Watching made for TV movies. Please, ask me."

"So what would make a serial killer stop killing for more than twenty years?"

Silence.

"Jim?"

"He, uh, the killer, uh…stopped for over twenty years?"

Had he told his old partner about the cold case he'd found? Levi wasn't sure now. He filled him in with vague details. No need to get bogged down.

"Huh… So the first case was—"

"Nearly thirty years ago," Levi told him.

"That's strange." Jim's voice was softer now, like he was holding the phone farther away from his ear. "Listen, Levi, this case, maybe you should…"

The call dropped.

Levi frowned. Then called back. It went straight to voice mail.

Was Jim having a heart attack? He was in good shape but it wasn't completely impossible. Levi didn't know what else besides sudden illness would have made him respond that way.

Surely if the killer himself had walked into the room Jim would have exclaimed, not tried to be subtle.

Levi mentally replayed their conversation. No, he had no idea what the problem was. But he didn't like it. The more he thought about it, the more he wondered about the medical-problem option.

He called 911 and asked for a welfare check with EMTs. If Jim was sick, they were the best ones to see about him. Did Levi dare go over there, knowing it was dangerous to be where Levi was right now, with a serial killer after him? Levi could be putting Jim in danger. Nah, he wouldn't do that to Jim. He'd wait and let the EMTs do their job and then talk to him later.

He'd already dragged one person down into this danger with him. And he wished with everything inside him that he could get her out. But it was too late.

"I just want to take her on a walk." Adriana tried again, having been told by Judah five seconds before that under no circumstances was she going anywhere. She'd been sitting in the house for hours. She'd left Judah outside in his car for a long time, then finally had gone outside a few minutes before to see if he wanted some coffee. He'd said yes and come inside.

It was then that she'd very calmly suggested that she might like to go for a walk.

He hadn't responded very calmly.

"And am I correct in saying that it was only earlier today you had someone following you and trying to kill you?"

He wasn't wrong. She exhaled.

"Fine. I can let her out to go to the bathroom in my own backyard, correct?"

"Of course." Judah stood from where he'd been sitting on the couch. "I'll go out with you."

Arguing with him wasn't going to get her anywhere, she knew, so she just nodded. "Okay, thank you." She wasn't foolish or shortsighted enough that she couldn't see that he was doing something nice, helping keep her safe.

She exhaled in the cool night air, walking around the yard as Blue did. Babe had done his business for the night already and refused to come outside with them.

Adriana was glad Blue had needed the trip out; she was beyond claustrophobic at this point and the fresh air was already helping her relax. As much as she could in this situation. Her house was on one of the edges of Raven Pass, and she could walk straight from her unfenced backyard—her dogs were trained to stay close to her—into the woods and hike endless miles of trails.

That thought had always comforted her, since she'd always loved the outdoors, but with the time she'd spent in the backcountry this week, unburying bodies and secrets, it felt like an eerie thought.

She wasn't so far removed from them as she wished she was.

"Almost done, sweetie?" she asked Blue, then looked around to find Judah. He was still in the yard, but farther away.

Blue trotted toward her.

"I'm heading in, okay?" she asked Judah.

He nodded. She headed for the door. She was almost there when Blue stopped, turned her head to the right and let out a long, guttural howl. Blue moved toward the side of the house and out of view.

Adriana frowned. Looked at where Blue had gone, then back at Judah. She wanted to be responsible, but she wasn't going to let her dog run away, either. She needed Blue.

"I've got to get her." She motioned with her hands. He was shaking his head, she could see that even though he was far away, and hurrying toward her now, but she needed to get to her dog.

She rounded the corner of the house. Blue was lying on the ground like she'd just alerted to a body. Adriana was wracked with guilt. Had she pushed her too hard? What else could have...?

"Hello."

She heard the voice at the same time as she felt a knife enter her side.

It was a woman.

And Adriana was fairly certain, as her vision started to swim in darker and darker shadows, that she was the one responsible for all the murders.

The serial killer had found her.

And Levi was nowhere nearby to save her.

SIXTEEN

"Did you guys get there yet?" Levi had called a friend, Isaac, who was an EMT with Raven Pass.

"We did. No one is home."

"I told you he hung up. Can you break down the door or something?" He felt a little absurd asking—no doubt Jim would laugh at him for his excessive worry, but he couldn't shake the concern.

"We got inside. No one is here."

Hard, cold dread fell like ice in his stomach.

If Jim hadn't had any kind of medical incident… He hadn't been taken by the killer, had he?

Levi's mind raced. That last conversation. Jim's strange reaction to what Levi had found. And then the line had gone dead.

All he could think of was Jim's wife... What was her name? Rosie?

Jim's wife must be around sixty years old. Yes, they were both in shape because they liked to hike together.

Surely Jim's wife wasn't...

Levi didn't care how absurd the idea was because it didn't really matter *who*, not at this point. All that mattered was that Jim was in trouble.

"I'll be right there," he told Isaac and hung up the phone.

He hurried to his car and called Judah on the way. On the off chance his crazy suspicion about Jim's wife was correct, he wanted his brother to be on the lookout and not let Adriana be alone with the sweet-looking woman if she came over. Even if he'd ruined his chances with her forever, he wanted her safe. It still felt like his job to protect her. While the phone rang, he navigated the dark roads, hating the fact that fall had stolen the daylight.

It wasn't quite all the way dark yet, but it was coming.

"Levi. Something has happened."

Judah's voice was gravel rough. And not hopeful.

"You heard about Jim already?" Levi asked.

"No." Silence.

"Judah. What?" Levi couldn't keep the tension from his voice.

"It's Adriana. She's gone."

"She's—" Levi couldn't breathe. It felt like he'd been gut punched. Except this time he'd never be able to catch a full breath again.

"They took her."

Alive. She is still alive. Not dead, like he'd assumed from his brother's phrasing.

"You were supposed to watch her!" His voice raised in volume and he didn't hold back any of his frustration.

"I was. She went to get her dog and I ran after her. When I rounded the house, something hit me over the head and knocked me over."

"How long were you passed out?" Levi was still biting back anger.

"Not long. A minute? Maybe not at all but I was disoriented. I'm sorry, Levi."

It could have been one minute or thirty. Judah had no way of knowing, and Levi knew it wasn't his brother's fault.

"I'm on my way," Levi said and hung up.

Levi swallowed hard and hit the gas, changing his course for Adriana's house. His old mentor could handle himself—at least Levi hoped so. But Adriana wasn't used to people like this and had no training for dealing with a killer.

Why had he left her at all? Oh, that's right, he'd been afraid of the feelings growing between them and scared he'd be right back where he'd been years ago, torn between his job and a woman. Except this time, he should have realized, there was a difference. Adriana hadn't asked him to give up anything. She hadn't complained. She hadn't questioned.

All she'd done was care.

And he'd let her down.

He bit back anger. Barely. "I'm on my way."

Her side hurt. It was strange, how one part of her body could throb in exhausting pain while the rest of her felt fine. Adriana would have thought all of her would hurt, but no, only the stab wound.

Was that how death was, too? she wondered.

"Walk faster." She was shoved forward, farther down the dark trail behind her house. She'd never walked very far this way before. They'd hiked in for a little while, ten minutes maybe, and then turned left. Adriana had always turned right, toward the developed trails. Left led to private land, so she'd never explored that way.

Because of that she had no concept of how hard or easy she would be to find.

Was there a body there from nearly thirty years ago? she wondered in passing. Was she going to be the new body?

Now her head throbbed, too, joining the stab wound in vying for her attention.

"Where are we going?" Was that her voice, groggy and wounded?

Please, God, let Blue lead them to where I am. She prayed as she waited for an answer. She'd issued a sharp command for Blue to get inside right after she'd been stabbed, and her dog had listened. Hopefully, Blue might lead a search party to her.

Levi? Would he be the one looking? Her SAR team?

She knew how this part went. The search grids. The agonizing minutes turning to hours, the knowledge that if a person wasn't found soon, exposure could kill.

All of that, plus this week's knowledge about humanity's depravity, was too much to handle. Adriana had seen death up close this week, what this woman's rage had done, all the lives it had ended.

She didn't want to be another casualty. She didn't want to be part of this killer's twisted plan.

"Why are you doing this?" Adriana asked. Her captor hadn't talked much, and Adriana didn't recognize her. The woman was older than she'd have pictured a killer, somewhere in her sixties, but fit. Smaller than Adriana, and built like a woman who spent her days hiking mountain trails.

And burying people on them.

All those victims—*this* woman had been responsible?

Still, she didn't answer. Instead, she shoved Adriana again, harder. She tripped on a root and fell to the ground. Pain knifed in her side, where her wound was, and she grabbed it with her hand and tried not to cry out. When she moved her hand away, there was fresh, sticky blood.

God, help me not die here, she prayed.

"If you're trying to be the biggest pain and slow me down so I let you go, it won't happen. I could kill you now, you know. I've killed many, many times."

How did you explain the feeling of hearing those words? Adriana wondered. There was no way to articulate the amount of evil in what should be a normal, pleasant voice. Or the way she could almost feel the...void behind her. Like the woman had traded in her humanity for something else altogether.

It was eerie. Terrifying.

Please don't let her kill me. She prayed, willing to beg God however much she needed to. Adriana wasn't ready to die. Too much of the last few years had been suffocated under thoughts of death. Robert's. The people she helped find. She needed a few years in full sunlight. In hope.

With Levi. Please, with Levi.

Please, not yet.

"I'll walk faster," Adriana promised, doing her best to get her legs to cooperate. They were heavy.

"Do that."

They hiked in silence. Another ten minutes, Adriana guessed. How far had they gone? It was hard to judge her pace when she knew she was walking more slowly than usual. More importantly, how fast could Levi hike it? And could Blue find them?

Was there still hope? Or was it really lost now?

She couldn't let herself think that, she reminded herself as she took more hurried steps into the darkness.

She had to believe there was still a chance. Levi knew she was missing by now; he had to. And she'd asked God to save her. Sometimes He allowed tragedy to strike, she knew that.

Yet sometimes God stepped in with miracles. And Adriana needed one of those right now.

Levi banged on the front door of Adriana's house with a closed fist, anger loaded and ready. It took Judah more than a minute to answer.

"Where is she?" Part of him needed to see that she was really gone, or he'd keep hoping maybe she'd just stepped into another room, maybe Judah hadn't seen her, maybe she was really fine.

Maybe he hadn't messed this all up. *Again*.

"I don't know. We were in the backyard, taking her dog for a walk."

It wasn't unreasonable, Levi knew that in his head. Still, he felt his fists clench. "You let her outside?"

"It was her backyard, Levi. I was with her. You couldn't lock her up forever."

No, he couldn't have. And with any other person in danger he'd have agreed with Judah. Quality of life was important and Adriana's had been smashed all to bits this week. He loved the idea of her outside in her own yard. Safe in the outside air. Finally relaxing a little.

Except he knew how this ended.

"When did she get away from you? How? Did someone come? Did she leave?"

Blue came trotting in from the living room, whining. She jumped up and put her paws on Levi's shoulders.

He didn't remember Blue ever jumping up on him before. She was far too well trained for that. Stress from her owner being missing?

"She went around the corner of the house." Judah nodded toward Blue. "The dog acted weird. Sort of howled and ran and then she followed and was gone." He shook his head. "I ran that way, and someone hit me. The dog came back, barreled right into me, actually, before I hit the ground, and then I passed out. When I got up, Adriana wasn't there."

Levi bent down, scratched Blue behind the ears and looked into her eyes, willing her to communicate with him somehow. Adriana did this all the time, right? She made it look so easy, but the truth was she was a talented woman. Talented and gorgeous and funny and brave.

He needed her to be okay.

"Please tell me something," he muttered at the dog.

"You're not talking to the dog, right? We'll find her, Levi. Let's go. I've already put a BOLO out for her and I've got everyone in the department looking for cars they don't recognize."

Levi shook his head. "Except that may not be our biggest danger."

Judah stilled. "We know the killer?"

"I'm not sure." Levi couldn't quite shrug, as it wasn't a casual shrugging situation, but he felt every bit as puzzled as his shoulders wanted to convey. "Jim's missing. I was on the phone with him, and he reacted really oddly to what I told him and then disappeared."

Blue whined and jumped up on Levi again, then ran toward the back of the house. Ran back. Again.

Levi frowned. "You want us to follow you."

"You're talking to the dog again," Judah said. "And the isn't *Lassie*."

Blue barked.

Levi nodded. "All right. Come with me, Judah. I'll fill you in on the way, but we're following the dog."

"Following..." Judah's voice trailed off, but Levi was already hot on Blue's heels as the husky ran ahead, then pawed at the back door.

This had to work. Levi swallowed hard against fear, desperate to do something to help Adriana. If she trusted her dogs, then...

Maybe he needed to do that, too.

Levi opened the door, said a quick prayer.

Without hesitation, the large white dog ran for the woods behind the house.

Woods. Levi swallowed hard and felt his chest compress. *Please, don't let me find her like every other woman I've found in the woods lately.*

Surely the killer wouldn't murder Adriana. Not if he—well, more likely *she*—was motivated by a sense of justice. If the killer was truly motivated by infidelity, by making that right somehow, then Adriana had done nothing wrong. She shouldn't be a target.

And wouldn't have been, if he hadn't gotten her involved in this case.

Shoving aside guilt that would do him

no good, he hurried after the dog. Prayed he wasn't too late. And that this actually worked.

Please, God, let this dog actually know what she's doing.

The glow of a light from a cabin would have been a welcome sight any other time, but right now it only added to Adriana's sense of foreboding.

She wasn't dead yet; that was a plus. However, the wet, sticky blood staining the side of her shirt served as a reminder that she could be. She had no idea how much blood she'd lost, no idea how much was too much. All she knew was that she was fighting waves of dizziness, but it could easily be panic.

"Now we wait for your boyfriend." The woman stepped ahead of Adriana and looked back at her with a look of bored hate. "Then you can die. Try to stay alive 'til he gets here. This works best if everyone knows how much their actions have made other people suffer."

The words reminded Adriana of what Levi had told her about the phone call, the fact that the person killing seemed to think they were doing something good, righting some kind of wrong. Is that what this person was referring to?

The door to the cabin pushed open easily against the woman's weight. There was no lock on the door, common in Alaskan cabins like this, something that should help Levi and anyone he might bring with him. *If* they got here. She'd lost track of how many turns they'd taken and there hadn't been a way to subtly mark their path with someone right behind her. At first she'd done her best by snapping twigs with her feet, but when the woman had become impatient, Adriana had decided that keeping her calm was her first priority.

She trusted Blue. If anyone could find her, Blue could. The question was whether or not Levi would trust the dog to do so, and if he could read her signals.

"Who is this? What did you do, Rosie?" a raspy male voice called from the corner of the room. A man sat in a chair, hands bound, tied to it. His feet were bound, too.

"Shut up, Jim."

Jim? She'd heard of Jim, hadn't she? Where had she heard that name lately?

"You did this, Jim. I didn't do this, *you* did."

The woman turned to the other corner. Adriana looked over there for the first time and saw another woman, not much younger than Adriana herself, tied up like the man. The only difference was that the man looked tired. Resigned. And the younger woman, who bore a resemblance to Rosie and Jim, looked terrified.

Adriana struggled to put the pieces together. Frowned.

Levi's old partner? Had his name been Jim?

"You did this, too, Jenny." Rosie turned toward the other corner and advanced. "You should have known better. *You* were raised better."

Now she spun around, back to Jim. "Unlike you, apparently."

"Rosie, I said I was sorry. A hundred times, I said it. I showed you every day. And it was over thirty years ago. And I stopped seeing her..."

Rosie shook her head. "Not. Soon. Enough."

Adriana watched as Jim's expression wavered, as understanding dawned.

"You...didn't..."

"She was the first to die. The others committed the same sin she did."

So Rosie had been the killer all those years ago.

But why...

Adriana watched the family drama unfolding before her, hoped for answers, but more than that, hoped for escape.

"You sit there." Rosie grabbed her arm, the one Adriana had kept pressed against her wound, and pulled her toward a chair.

Adriana sat. Put her hand back against her side. Blood stuck to her skin.

"Why did you stop?" Adriana asked, knowing she had little to lose by at least getting answers.

Rosie jerked her head toward the young woman. "I spent years raising her. Pouring all my energy into raising the perfect daughter." Her face contorted into a sneer. "Only to have my daughter follow in her father's footsteps with her bad moral choices. Dating a married man! Just like that other woman who wrecked my marriage. No better than she was. Then I realized I could never stop killing. That there would always be more people who had been unfaithful or helped someone else be unfaithful, people who needed to die."

Wrong as infidelity was, the woman was sick. Adriana felt nauseous as her stomach churned.

"Why me, though? I haven't done anything wrong."

Although, yes, it was madness that the killer was justifying her actions, Adriana had to keep her talking if she wanted to live. At least that was her theory.

"You kept interfering. You and your boyfriend."

He wasn't her boyfriend, Adriana wanted to say, but denying it was hardly going to help her now, was it?

Besides, she loved him. There was no point in denying that now. Either to herself or anyone else.

She. Loved. Him.

The woman grabbed a rope and started to tie Adriana up as she continued, "Seeing you die will hurt him. Which will hurt you." Rosie turned to Jim, her husband, and glared.

Okay, maybe knowing they weren't a couple could help, much as that truth hurt Adriana. "We aren't together. Killing me gets you nothing."

Rosie shrugged. "Maybe, maybe not. But I've been watching. I see the way he looks at you. Anyway, he will want to save you. And when he gets here, he will die while my husband watches and sees what his sin has cost *everyone*."

Adriana kept quiet.

There didn't seem to be anything more to say.

SEVENTEEN

The dark tangles of the woods surrounded them as they hiked on into the night. Blue looked back at Levi now and then and he nodded at her, trying to convey somehow that he was trusting her. Adriana would know how to do this. She'd led countless searches.

Levi looked at Blue. Swallowed hard. She was a regular search dog, too, wasn't she? Because he couldn't handle the possibility that she'd caught a cadaver scent. Adriana had to be alive. He stopped walking abruptly, tried to catch his breath.

"What's wrong?" Judah asked from behind him, having had to stop suddenly to avoid hitting him.

Levi shook his head. The words brought

up such a big fear, he didn't even want to say it aloud.

"She'll be okay."

But his brother couldn't promise that and they both knew it.

Blue whined and trotted ahead again, then came back. Levi was fairly sure this was the same dog she used for all her searches. With that thought in mind to give him the little bit of hope he needed, he moved forward.

He tripped on a root at one point, but stayed focused. Only when they got off the trail did he start to worry.

"You sure about this?" Judah asked.

No, Levi wasn't sure at all. But Blue seemed pretty confident. He hadn't seen her sniffing the ground, like he would picture a search dog doing, but from the little bit Adriana had explained to him, it seemed like the dogs were able to find scent in air. So maybe it didn't have to be exactly what he was picturing.

He needed to trust the dog.

As he walked, questions started to nudge his heart.

Was this anything like trusting God? Following a path that didn't make sense to him, going through things like he'd gone through in the past? Why was he willing to trust a dog, but not the God who had created him and the universe?

Because he was mad. He knew the answer right away. He'd grown up following Jesus, tried to do his best in his marriage, and it had still fallen apart. Now he walked around with his own kind of scarlet letter, at least in some parts of the Christian community, because he was divorced. But his church and friends had never made him feel that way.

So did anyone judge him at all? Or did it just feel that way?

And either way, was God to blame?

No, he knew as he hiked through the darkness. God was not. He was without fault, without blame. He'd been there all the time, waiting for Levi to come to Him with the heartache he'd gone through, and instead of drawing closer to Him, Levi had pushed away.

Why had it taken the thought of losing Adriana, just when he was starting to believe in second chances, for him to realize it?

God, I'm sorry. Help me trust You. Help me find her.

It may not have been the most eloquent prayer. But as he saw glimmers of light in the distance, like light from cabin windows, he could feel something inside him lighten as well.

Hope. Hope that maybe God had been working everything out, even still was.

Please let that mean that she's alive, he prayed again as the shape of a cabin became more distinct in the darkness.

"Blue, come."

The dog did, went to him obediently, even though he could tell she could clearly smell what she'd been chasing, from the way she danced on her hind legs and whined.

"And be quiet."

She stopped making noise. Levi frowned. How well trained was this dog?

"What's your plan?" Judah asked him, and Levi felt himself stand taller. Shoulders back. For once, his older brother had asked *him* that question. Of course, this time Levi wasn't sure he had a plan, and could have maybe used his brother's help. But he wasn't going to admit that now.

"I think I should stay out of sight for now," Judah offered.

Yes. That was a solid plan. Levi nodded like he'd already thought that through. "You stay out of sight. I'll go in and try to get her."

"You won't be able to just storm in and yank her out. Besides, didn't you say your old partner may be in there, too?"

True. So they'd have an officer going in through the door, one outside. Two hostages. One killer. He liked the odds. The hostages were on his side, but it was still not without risk. If Adriana was still alive, it wasn't because this was a killer who showed mercy. It was because she was somehow worth more to them alive than dead.

That made him uncomfortable, to not understand what they were planning. Also, what shape would Adriana be in? She was a fit woman. If she hadn't managed to escape at her house, then she'd potentially been knocked out, drugged, or worse. He had to factor that in as well.

Levi's mouth was dry and the taste of fear was overwhelming. Adrenaline buzzed down his arms, through his veins. He needed her to be all right.

He needed to do the best he could for her.

He crept toward the cabin, quietly. His feet fell on the ground of the Alaskan woods carefully as he made his way closer.

Blue walked alongside him.

The husky. Did he bring her or not? Adriana wouldn't like her dog being in danger and she might make an impulsive decision if it seemed like Blue was. On the other hand, his chances of being able to save her were greater with the animal for help.

The risk was worth it.

"Don't make me regret this," he whispered to the dog.

They moved as one toward the cabin.

He could hear voices from inside. A woman was talking. The killer?

"If you had never been unfaithful..."

"Rosie, please." Jim's voice.

Levi had never wished so badly to have been wrong, but his partner's wife was the killer. It sickened him to imagine the bodies he'd looked at over the years, to know that it had been her evil and hatred that had ended people's lives.

A gunshot suddenly rang out.

Levi had no more time.

He burst through the closed door of the cabin, the dog at his heels, and hoped that Blue would have some inkling as to how to handle herself in this kind of situation.

"Levi!" Adriana yelled, and as Rosie turned her head to watch the dog, Levi tackled her. The gun fell from her hands and clattered to the floor. As he wrestled her arms behind her back and reached for the cuffs at his side, he looked around.

His assessment had been mostly right. Three hostages. Jim, Adriana and a young woman he didn't recognize.

"Their daughter," Adriana said. Levi nodded but couldn't see if anyone had been shot.

Rosie screamed and fought him, but he finished getting the handcuffs on. "Rosie Johnson, you are under arrest." He continued with her Miranda rights, surprised that his voice was steady as he recited them from memory. She would spend the rest of her life in jail, and the area would finally be free from her terrorizing people and taking some perverted form of justice into her own hands.

Levi's heart beat hard in his chest, but he took slow, deep breaths. It was over. They'd arrested her. He could breathe again.

"No!" Adriana's shout behind him jerked his eyes upward in time to see his old partner, Jim, reach for the gun and aim it at Adriana.

"Jim." Levi's voice was low. Full of disbelief.

Rosie had been behind the killings, right?

"She is still my wife," Jim said with a gasp and Levi noticed for the first time that Jim was the one who had been shot. Blood spattered the right side of his chest. Maybe a fatal wound, maybe not. But enough to slow him down. Not enough to necessarily make him less accurate firing a couple shots of his own. Rosie must have shot him right before Levi had come in. That was the gunshot he had heard.

"Don't do it, Jim." Levi kept his own voice calm. From beside Adriana, Blue growled.

"Make your dog stay put or I shoot her, too. And I hate killing dogs."

Adriana looked down at Blue. "Stay," she told her calmly.

Too calmly. Her voice was quiet, like she was losing strength. Levi looked over at

her. The corner of her shirt, on her side…
Was it darker than the rest? And if so, was
it a shadow or a bloodstain?

With wavering hands, Jim lifted the gun
back to Adriana. Trained it straight on her.

"You need to forget this happened, Levi.
Bury it somewhere in your memory." Jim
was panting between words now—the
gunshot must have damaged several or-
gans inside him. Or the blood loss was
just too much because Levi could see him
fading away. Desperate sadness at losing a man who had been a mentor to him
fought against some kind of relief. At this
point Jim was at least guilty of attempted
murder, and it might be getting worse. He
hated the idea of his friend in jail.

He doubted he'd have to worry about
that.

"Jim. Put the gun down. It's not who
you are."

The window behind Jim. Levi frowned.
Did he see something? A flicker of light?
Movement?

Judah. It was his brother. Levi felt his

shoulders relax even as he kept his eyes trained on the man holding a gun within ten feet of the woman he suddenly realized he loved more than anything on earth.

"Put. It. Down," Levi insisted. As he finished speaking, the glass in the window behind Jim crashed. Jim jerked up the gun and swiveled his head around, so Levi rushed him. He'd come within a foot when Jim leaped back and swung the gun at Levi.

"Levi!" Adriana yelled, and he heard the noise of her chair moving, scraping against the wood floor of the cabin, but there was nothing she could do, nowhere she could go.

No, this was all on Levi until Judah could get back around to the side of the house. The cabin window was too high for him to climb into, but Judah had been brilliant to cause a distraction the way he had and trust Levi to do something with it. It was a kind of teamwork that he couldn't remember having experienced in a long time. They were equals who still needed each other.

Having a partner sometimes wasn't so bad. And he wasn't going to let his brother down now by getting shot and messing this up.

Levi lunged toward his former partner, as he tried to fight him off. Levi jerked hard one final time, tightening his grip on the man's arm as he pushed it down. The gun fell to the floor, again, and this time Levi kicked it to the side, out of the way.

Now. *Now* it was over.

Judah ran in the door, ran over to him. "You got him?"

Levi nodded. "Got him."

"I called the PD. They're sending backup, lots of it. They should be here soon."

Then it would truly be over.

Jim breathed hard, losing strength as Levi kept him restrained but cuffed him carefully with the handcuffs Judah handed him. He could hear the man crying.

Jim had made bad choices, most of

which Levi probably didn't know about, and it would be a struggle to forgive him, Levi knew. But he could ask God to help him with that.

At least he had his life ahead of him. The woman he loved...

"This is your fault!" Rosie screamed in Jim's direction.

The woman in the corner, tied to the chair, was crying, too.

"And you are?" Judah walked over and asked her.

"Jenny. I'm their—their daughter..." She trailed off, started to cry again.

"She started killing after Jim had an affair," Adriana said. "And then stopped killing while she raised her daughter."

"I thought I could stop! I thought I could make it right by raising my daughter to be a good woman, not the kind of man stealing..." Her voice trailed off.

"She stopped until her daughter made the same mistake as her father, by seeing a married person." Adriana's voice was quiet.

Levi looked at all of them. His former partner, struggling to breathe. The sobbing woman in the corner.

The angry murderer still sitting on the floor.

And then back at Adriana. The shadow at her side was darker now. There was no more denial. "You're bleeding." He felt himself struggle to breathe as panic overwhelmed him. He had to get her out of here now, back to Raven Pass, to a doctor.

Because he hadn't come this far to lose her now.

Adriana remembered falling asleep, as consciousness played at the corners of her mind. Her side hurt, ached. Throbbed.

She had woken up on a stretcher, in the woods, and had the sense that she was being carried through the forest, probably by the backup that Judah had called.

Thoughts crowded her mind.

"Blue?" she remembered asking.

"She's fine. I've got her." Levi's voice. Calm and reassuring.

She'd fallen back asleep, let the darkness take her.

Now she blinked her way toward the light again. The bright fluorescents of the hospital room where she appeared to be were harsh.

There was Levi. Standing beside her.

"You're awake," he said and smiled.

She loved him, she realized again. She'd never loved someone quite this way before. It was different than the love she'd shared with her fiancé. Not because she'd loved Robert any less, but because they'd had a relationship at a time in her life when she hadn't known as much about loss and the cost of love. In some strange way, loss had taught her to care more deeply.

"I love you," he said to her, quietly.

She blinked.

He grinned wider. "You okay? Did you hear me? I love you, Adriana. And if I'm bad at relationships, I'll work on that, and I won't give up, because I love you. And that's not what love does."

She smiled back at him. "I love you, too," she said to him as she met his eyes.

They stayed that way, staring, for what seemed like minutes but could have been seconds. Her perception of time was still off.

She frowned.

"I'm in the hospital?"

"The doctors wanted to check your stab wound. You needed a little bit of blood, but you're going to be okay. I'm so glad. I love you so much."

Adriana nodded, tried to sit up a little against the pillows.

"I learned some things about the case," he started, then paused. "Did you want to know this now?" Adriana nodded, but also suppressed a small laugh. This was what life with Levi would be like. They'd be talking about something serious, talking about their love for each other, and then he'd bring up a case. She knew it as surely as she knew anything else. And it was fine with her. She wouldn't change the way he was for anything.

"What did you learn?" she asked.

"I sent a team down to try to see if there was a body near where the very first one was discovered. Outside the town of Hope."

"Did they find something?"

He nodded. "Yes. Fifteen feet away from the site of the original body was another."

They were the same measurements, same MO of having two bodies buried near each other. That was a strange element of Rosie's MO they'd probably never have an explanation for, but it had been consistent through each body Adriana knew of.

"Anything else?" She could see that there was in the way he looked at her, with his eyes lit up. He nodded again.

"The body we found this time was a woman who was from the town of Hope. She appears to have been killed before the first body we found there." His face turned serious. "She was the woman Jim had an affair with. Rosie admitted to it once she was down at the station. She seems to have no desire to plead innocent, which is driving her lawyer crazy. She was only too happy to confirm what we knew and tell us some information we didn't know yet."

"That's why we were run off the Seward Highway the other day," Adriana commented. "Because if we had started talking to that victim's friends, the investigation would have uncovered Jim's affair. Then we would have started asking questions of Jim. And his wife."

"And we would have figured out it was her," Levi confirmed.

Adriana closed her eyes. What a broken world they lived in, she thought. And yet a world full of good things, too. She never wanted to forget that and let the bad weigh her down. There was always a glimmer of hope to be found.

"She also told me that Jim met the woman he had an affair with at a coffee shop."

"That's why Rosie found her victims there?"

Levi nodded. "Women who were cheating or helping someone else cheat. Always taken from a coffee shop as a kind of sick memorial to what Rosie's husband had done to her with his betrayal."

Another detail of the case explained. Adriana had wondered.

Sick, sick woman.

Adriana shook her head, still overwhelmed with sadness. She looked away from Levi. A few minutes passed in heavy silence.

"Adriana?"

She turned to him, noting the seriousness in his voice.

"I don't want to date you."

She raised her eyebrows, waiting for him to elaborate. He'd told her five minutes ago that he loved her. And now...

"I want to get married."

If she hadn't been lying down already, she'd have needed to sit. The words stunned her, but filled her with more hope and happiness than she could explain.

"You want to marry me?"

"I want to marry you," Levi said again. "Will you please do me the honor of becoming my wife?"

He was down on one knee now, and in her mind Adriana knew the scene looked ridiculous, with her on a hospital bed, under a pile of blankets, and him down on one knee.

"I don't have a ring yet. I've been in the middle of this crazy case, see. I'll get a ring, though, as soon as we can. You can pick it out, or I can. I think I could do a pretty good job. I love you, Adriana. That's what matters to me..."

Adriana pushed herself farther into a sitting position.

"Levi?"

"Yes?"

"The ring doesn't matter." Well, it would be exciting. And she'd love seeing it as a sparkling reminder of promises on her finger, but it didn't matter as much as Levi himself.

He looked at her. Eyebrows raised. Anticipating her answer.

"I would love to marry you, Levi Wicks." She laughed as he reached out his arms and hugged her in the gentlest way possible, careful not to press against her wound.

"I know it's fast, but we've known each other for years." He nodded. "I know we can do this, Adriana. We make a good team. And we'll make a good team together."

It was another vote of confidence—Levi being convinced that they would make this work, that their love would only grow stronger. She loved him even more for it.

"Are you sure?" His eyes flickered with a tiny hint of vulnerability. "It would be forever."

"Forever with you is exactly what I want," she assured him, and she put her hands on either side of his face, cradling his jaw, as she leaned forward into his kiss.

EPILOGUE

Never had Levi been prouder than at the sight of both of his brothers dressed in suits, for him. Ryan was performing the wedding ceremony, and Judah was his best man.

Neither he nor Adriana had wanted a long engagement, so as soon as she was fully healed, they'd started to plan the wedding. It was just over three months since that day in the hospital when he'd asked her to marry him.

And he loved her more than ever.

Levi looked at his older brothers and smiled. But as he caught Judah's eye he smiled a little wider.

They had never explicitly talked about Judah's tendency to treat Levi like he was perpetually in need of his help, but somehow after that night at the cabin, when Judah had come through for him without making him feel less than capable, everything had turned out okay.

He stood at the front of the church, eyes fixed on the door at the back of the room. In a few minutes, Adriana would come through those doors. He couldn't believe that only half an hour or less stood between him and forever.

Despite his past hurts, today was only a celebration. Of the fact that they'd survived the hardest case he'd ever worked, of their love and that he'd found a teammate for life.

The doors opened. She walked in, looking beautiful in a dress that highlighted her curves in a subtle way that he found so beautiful.

That word. *Beautiful.* It was everything about her, but not just her. It was everything about their story.

He'd stopped trusting God after heartache, then had finally tentatively tried again. And God had blessed him beyond his wildest dreams.

"I love you," he whispered to Adriana as she came closer.

Her eyes met his. They flickered, full of hope.

Again, that word. *Beautiful*.

"I love you, too."

They were the best words Levi had ever heard.

* * * * * *

Dear Reader,

If there is one thing humans struggle with, it's trust. We wonder if we should trust ourselves, our friends and even the God who created us. Sometimes that's because of our past circumstances, which is what Adriana struggled with in this book. Because of a loss she'd experienced earlier in life, she wondered if God was really good, which shook her trust in Him.

Whatever has happened in your life, God does not change. He is good now as He always has been, and this is what Adriana learns in her story. Levi, likewise, has to learn to trust God and lean into a relationship with Him with his whole heart. It's not always intentional that my hero and heroine learn similar lessons, but that's usually how it ends up. Want to know a secret? It's often a lesson I'm learning in my own life.

I hope you enjoyed this second book in the Raven Pass Search and Rescue series. If you ever want to visit Raven Pass, which is, sadly, fictional, the next best thing is to visit Girdwood, Alaska. It's set back against the mountains near Turnagain Arm in south central Alaska, and it is a beautiful place. If you find yourself with a chance to visit, I think you'll love it. And if not, keep joining me for more books set in Raven Pass.

As always, I love hearing from readers. Please feel free to reach out on facebook at facebook.com/sarahvarlandauthor, or email me at sarahvarland@gmail.com. Thank you for giving me some hours of your time to tell you this story.

Sarah Varland